Simon Raven was  as educated at Charte ge where he read Cla he army as a regular nt Infantry and saw se e commanded a Rifl is commission and to l, *The Feathers of Death*, was published in 1959. Since then he has written many reviews, general essays and plays for radio and television as well as the scripts for a number of successful television series including *Edward and Mrs Simpson* and *Love in a Cold Climate* plus a host of novels. The highly acclaimed ALMS FOR OBLIVION sequence has been referred to as 'a latter-day Waugh report on another generation of Bright Young Things', and has been compared favourably with the *romans fleuves* of Anthony Powell and C. P. Snow. With the publication in 1984 of *Morning Star* he began a new novel series under the title THE FIRST-BORN OF EGYPT. It is a sequel to ALMS FOR OBLIVION. Simon Raven lives and works in Deal, Kent.

By the same author

Novels

The Feathers of Death
Brother Cain
Doctors Wear Scarlet
The Roses of Picardie
Close of Play
An Inch of Fortune
September Castle

The ALMS FOR OBLIVION sequence,
in chronological order:

Fielding Gray
Sound the Retreat
The Sabre Squadron
The Rich Pay Late
Friends in Low Places
The Judas Boy
Places Where They Sing
Come Like Shadows
Bring Forth the Body
The Survivors

THE FIRST-BORN OF EGYPT sequence

Morning Star
The Face of the Waters
Before the Cock Crow
New Seed for Old
Blood of My Bone

Belles-Lettres

The English Gentleman
Boys Will be Boys
The Fortunes of Fingel
The Old School

Plays

Royal Foundation and Other Plays

Autobiography

Shadows on the Grass
The Old Gang
Bird of Ill Omen

SIMON RAVEN

In the Image
of God

The First-born of Egypt: Volume 6

GraftonBooks

A Division of HarperCollins*Publishers*

GraftonBooks
A Division of HarperCollins*Publishers*,
77–85 Fulham Palace Road,
Hammersmith, London W6 8JB

Published by GraftonBooks 1991
9 8 7 6 5 4 3 2 1

First published in Great Britain by
Frederick Muller, an imprint of
Century Hutchinson Ltd, 1990

A CIP catalogue record for this book
is available from the British Library

ISBN 0-586-20021-5

Printed in Great Britain by
HarperCollinsManufacturing Glasgow

Set in Times

So God created man in his own image, in the image of God created he him; male and female created he them.

Genesis, Ch. I, verse 27

Demiurgus (Greek), in the language of Platonists, means that mysterious agent which made the world, and all that it contains . . .

Dictionary of Phrase and Fable,
by the Revd Dr E. Cobham
Brewer of Trinity Hall, Cambridge,
12th Edition, p. 219

Demogorgon . . . [auth. Statius (*Thebais*)] 'the most high of the triple universe, whom it is unlawful to know' . . . perhaps a mistake for Demiurgus, the Creator.

> The *Oxford Companion to Classical
> Literature*, Compiled and Edited
> by Sir Paul Harvey, Third Edition,
> p. 139

Demogorgon. A terrible deity, whose very name was capable of producing the most horrible effects.

> The Revd Dr Brewer's *Dictionary
> of Phrase and Fable (v. supra)*,
> p. 219

PART ONE
The Magus

'So you see,' said the Marchioness Canteloupe, who was nine months gone with child, to the elderly companion with whom she walked on the winter beach, 'so you see, Auntie Flo, Marius Stern arrived too late at Brindisi. Whatever happened had already happened, and he had nothing to do with it. So there was no test, no challenge; no taint of evil, no signal of grace.'

'That's all very well,' said Auntie Flo (who was everyone's aunt and nobody's). She took Theodosia Canteloupe by the arm and led her to the edge of the many-sounding sea. 'There must have been some indication of how the matter might have gone if Marius had got to Brindisi in time to take part.'

'Piero Caspar, who escorted him there, is very doubtful. On balance, his judgement is that Marius would have played Judas had he met Jeremy in time. But there were occasions on which Marius seemed to be tending the other way – and in any case at all, as we have told each other *ad nauseam*, Marius simply did not meet Jeremy in time. Marius was here with you over Christmas, Auntie Flo; you're the last of us to have seen him; did he give you any clues about how he might have behaved . . . had he arrived in Brindisi in time to confront Jeremy Morrison?'

'None. (Breathe in deeply, dear; sea air is good for the baby.) He concentrated entirely on making my Christmas the happiest I can remember for sixty years. He was very careful to suppress his excitement at the prospect of joining Jeremy Morrison in Greece on 28 December, because he did not wish to hurt me, to let me realize that

9

he was simply aching to be gone. But of course there was no question of my being hurt. Of course a boy of that age wants to be off with his friend. I was only touched that for ten whole days he took enormous trouble to try and hide the fact. He gave me one very appropriate Christmas present, Thea: he gave me love.'

'And then left immediately.'

'He cried when he left. (Watch out for that wave, Thea: pregnant women should not get their feet sopping wet.) He said, "I must go, because Jeremy is my favourite person in the whole world. I wish it could be you," he said: "I love you more than I love Jeremy . . . but he is my favourite person, which is different."'

'And yet this Jeremy . . . his favourite person . . . is the one whom he would have betrayed.'

'*Might* have betrayed. We shall never know,' said Auntie Flo, dragging Thea back from the fractious foam, and wheeling her in the direction of Sandy Lodge, which was half a mile back along the beach towards Burnham-on-Sea.

'Who knows that he's gone?' said Theodosia. 'Raisley Conyngham, the slee dominee? These days Marius does not do much without Raisley Conyngham's imprimatur.'

'Raisley, the dark Angel, eh? I never much cared for him when I used to meet him at the races in the old days.'

'If only he confined himself to race courses. It is his presence as a senior and respected master at Marius' school that bothers me.'

'That bothers all of us,' said Auntie Flo. 'For once, however, I think Marius has acted independently of Raisley and his wishes. On 22 December, an air ticket to Corfu via Athens arrived from Jeremy, with a note to say that he wanted to make up for past disappointments in this line and was now inviting Marius to meet him in Corfu on 28 December and accompany him on a brief tour of the Peloponnese. There was also a note for me: it said that Jeremy would ensure that Marius was back here in Burnham by 10 January, in good time to return to school on the fifteenth.'

'So Jeremy was not exactly asking your permission, but he was deferring to you?'

'Civil enough. Not many people bother to defer to a penniless old woman. Not really penniless,' said Auntie Flo, nuzzling briefly against Theodosia's shoulder, 'because of you, my darling, but penniless before the world, which you forbid me to tell of your kindness. Anyway, Marius has his own money since his father died, and quite a lot of it, so that it would really be absurd for me to think in terms of having charge of him, or giving permission for him to accept invitations.'

'Only just,' said Theodosia Canteloupe sharply.

'Don't be prickly, girl. Even though Marius is the father of the child you are carrying, he is still under sixteen. But as I was saying, he has his own money and goes his own way – except that he normally consults Raisley first. On this occasion he did not. Raisley lives quite near here, as you very well know – at Ullacote by Timberscombe, only half an hour from Minehead. Marius could easily have got in touch with him personally, or simply have telephoned him. He did neither. He put the ticket in his pocket, and he said, "I must not refuse him, Auntie Flo, or he would be upset. He's had a lot to upset him lately, with that horrid business in Australia; and although he's over that now, I think I must go." "Yes, darling," I said: "I think so too." So he spent Christmas loving me and trying to pretend he didn't really want to leave on the twenty-eighth. Then he came out with the truth while he was saying goodbye, and a very endearing truth it was. But in all of this, no mention of the matter to Raisley (as far as I know, and I know quite far) nor any mention of Raisley to me.

'This time,' said Auntie Flo, 'he is not in any way under the instructions of Raisley Conyngham.'

'Good. But I still don't quite trust his affection for Jeremy. People should not feel affection for Jeremy.'

'You did. Your sister did.'

'We should not have done,' Theodosia said; 'he was worthless.'

'Between you, you saved him. By setting up that journey from Ithaca.* You two set it up – *you* told me. It has been the salvation of him – everybody says so though I don't quite understand what happened.'

'At the end of his voyage, he believed that he had somehow come to be present at the death of the poet Virgil, in Brindisi nearly 2,000 years ago, and that he was able to serve and comfort the poet as he died. He suffered great pain for the sake of Virgil – or so it seemed to him – in order to stop his poetry being stolen by a rival. He redeemed himself.'

'But only in a dream?'

'Say rather . . . in a vision.'

'And what,' said Auntie Flo, 'has he done with himself since having this vision?'

'He went into Norfolk,' said Theodosia. 'He gave great pleasure to his father and an old family servant by staying at Luffham for Christmas. He gave it out to his friends that he would be there over the New Year and until further notice – but as you and I and Marius now know, he left for Corfu to meet Marius. You say that he has promised to have Marius back here by 10 January. Will he come here with him?'

* See *Blood of My Bone* by Simon Raven (Muller/Century Hutchinson, 1989 or GraftonBooks)

'As to that, we shall see,' said Auntie Flo. 'He is welcome to spend a night or two in Sandy Lodge – if it's still there. Look, Thea. The dunes are withdrawing further and further. At certain seasons Sandy Lodge is an island at high tide. Look now. We must hurry, lest we be cut off from our own front door.'

'Homer called it "Sandy Pylos",' said Jeremy Morrison to Marius Stern, as they walked on the stone promenade above the stony beach of the Bay of Navarino.

'I have actually read the *Odyssey* myself. Or much of it.'

'If you know so much, tell me where Homer's "Sandy Pylos" really was.'

'The Palace,' said Marius, green eyes glistening at Jeremy, 'was some miles north. The old harbour was much nearer – under that Venetian castle at the top end of the bay. That is where Telemachus disembarked to meet Nestor "on the sands of the sea". I did the passage with Mr Conyngham last spring.'

Marius looked across the bay and sighed.

'Such a deep sigh,' Jeremy said: 'for Raisley Conyngham or Homer?'

'For both.'

'I know a chap,' Jeremy said, 'a very nice chap, who went up to Oxford to read the classics for four years and spent his entire time reading Homer. He read nothing else whatever. He got a poor third in Mods and failed Greats absolutely flat. Well worth it, he said. He knew most of the *Iliad* and all of the *Odyssey* by heart.'

'Sandy Pylos,' Marius said. '"Pray now, stranger from the sea, to the Lord Poseidon, for his is the feast whereon you have chanced in coming hither." That is what old Nestor said to Telemachus. I remember Mr Conyngham drew my particular attention to that passage. "Always be

13

polite to the God of any Feast which you may attend," he said, "and also to the *Genius Loci.*"'

'Good advice,' said Jeremy. 'Raisley was full of it, as I recall, when I sat under him at school some years back. But they seem to think he is giving *you* a certain amount of extra advice, special tutelage, which is not so wholesome. To put it another way, Raisley does not, unlike my chum at Oxford, confine himself to Homer. He is just as likely, some of your friends think, to be teaching you in the tradition of Hermes Trismegistus.'

'Magic?' said Marius. 'I have learned no magic from Raisley Conyngham.'

'What have you learned?'

'How to write Latin and Greek verses. How to translate from Latin and Greek texts. How to appreciate what I read in them, while always remaining critical of it.'

'I can't fault that. What else has he taught you?'

'Lots of things. That this town we are in was built by the French after the Battle of Navarino. That a party of Spartans held out bravely against the Athenians in 425 B.C. on the island opposite us, which guards the bay and is called Sphacteria. That the island is said to have been the scene for Byron's *Corsair*. Raisley, you see, is not concerned merely with words, with translating this way and that. He explains, minutely, the history and topography which frame ancient literature.'

'Yes. Although he was away quite a lot when I was at school, I remember him as a fine, broad teacher. Therefore a great power for evil, Marius, as well as for good. What is Raisley teaching you apart from classics?'

'To play the world's game.'

Jeremy turned about. They walked back down the promenade towards the Turkish castle, which sat under a low ridge near the south end of the port.

'And my knowledge of the world's game tells me this,'

14

said Marius; 'it is bad form, if not actually against the rules, to ask too many questions – particularly of an invited guest.'

'In Homer they were always asking questions of their guests.'

'Only if he were uninvited; and even then they were confined to the necessary minimum, to establish the guest's identity and provenance.'

'But questions about other people were allowed, to any amount. I am questioning you about another person, about Raisley Conyngham.'

'Yes; but about Raisley Conyngham in his relation to me. You surely haven't had me fly all the way to the terrain of Homer . . . first to Untoiling Scheria and now to Sandy Pylos . . . just to ask tedious questions about my intercourse with my pedagogue.'

'I have brought you here so that I may be the first to show these places to you. Raisley has only told you about them. Now you are seeing them, with me.'

'I wish we could go on seeing them for ever. This afternoon we shall go to Methoni?'

'Yes,' said Jeremy.

'And tomorrow to Areopolis and Vatheia and Gytheion.'

'And then Monemvasia. Black Sparta and Sweet Argos, Epidauros and Tiryns and Mycenae. Frankish towers and Christian tombs and Turkish castles and the Shrines of the Old Gods.'

'And there will be no more talk of Raisley Conyngham?'

'None. Until we are back with your Auntie Flo, making you ready to return to school. And then, I am afraid you will find, the talk of Raisley Conyngham will begin once more.'

'I shall be with him at school,' said Marius, 'learning from him.'

'That is why the talk will begin again, though most of it, of course, not in your presence. Your friends will be asking each other what is the most important thing you are learning from Raisley. They do not think it is Latin verse or the geography of the Peloponnese.'

For a while the tall fair thin boy and the even taller fair and fattish man walked on in silence. Then Marius turned his face up towards his friend's and said:

'I have just told you myself. He is teaching me the world's game.'

'There are as many versions of that,' said Jeremy Morrison, 'as there are of fives or football. What interests your friend is which version he is teaching you and under what code he is instructing you to play it. And now – no more of him, I promise, until we return to England. This fortress is Byzantine with Ottoman additions or Venetian with Turkish additions; I forget which. But I do remember that there is a brilliantly sited hotel just underneath it. The hotel stands partly in the bay itself, and some of its rooms have windows from which you may look straight down into the waters –

> . . . magic casements, opening on the foam
> Of perilous seas in faery lands forlorn.'

'Oh Jeremy . . . Why are we staying in the dreary old Xenia Nestor instead of in this enchanted hotel?'

'Because, dear boy, the dreary old Xenia Nestor is warm and dry and feeds one after a fashion. This enchanted hotel, as you call it, provides lukewarm bath water and damp sheets, as I once found out at the cost of a horrid bout of bronchitis. Shrewd players of the world's game give such places a wide berth. This one, as you can

16

see now we are coming closer, is in any case shut for the winter.'

Carmilla Salinger came from Cambridge to be with her sister in her labour. As soon as she arrived the tide rose and Sandy Lodge was surrounded by the sea.

'Thrilling,' said Theodosia.

'Not if you start and the doctor can't get through,' Carmilla said.

'Flo was a nurse during the war,' said Theodosia. 'I'd sooner have her than anyone else. That's why I'm here. I couldn't have borne a room in a hospital – all that hygienic fuss, and Canty lowering about like a ghoul, and all the left-wing nurses hating me.'

'You could have had it at home.'

'I'm having it here.' ·

'Suppose Flo gets drunk?' said Carmilla.

'Suppose it's got two heads. Drunk or sober, Flo would kill it. In a hospital they'd keep the beastly thing going. I had enough trouble with my stepson, Sarum. I don't want any more freaks about the house.'

'These days,' said Carmilla, musing and not reproaching, 'you're meant to preserve freak babies. Once upon a time they didn't bother, but now they do.'

'I wonder why.'

'It seems there's now something called the "sanctity of life" – a kind of monsters' charter. Its real object is to annoy and inconvenience normal people.'

'No monsters' charter in this house,' said Auntie Flo, who was entering with a tray of vodka, toast and caviar, 'never you fear. I learned all I need to know in that line in the Red Cross in Greece, before everyone got so sanctimonious. No food or medicine to spare for geriatrics or stumer babies, you see – so they just got their quietus.

17

And lucky to get it, when one considers what everyone else in Greece had to put up with just then.'

'How did they get it?' Theodosia enquired.

'One can always find a way when the time comes,' said Auntie Flo, 'if one keeps one's wits about one. Anyhow, I've telephoned Doctor La Soeur for some reminders, and he's told me about one or two modern tricks which you have to use now that there's so many busybodies about. So *that's* all right. And now eat these nourishing black balls, girl, paid for with your own money, and when your pains come on, just yell for Auntie Florence.'

'A snake,' said Marius: 'see where it goes. That yellow streak in the centre of the floor.'

Marius and Jeremy were sitting in the theatre at Epidaurus, half-way up the semi-circular tiers of stone seats.

'Do you see it?' Marius said.

'I see it. It is moving off the floor now, and away into the woods. No doubt Raisley Conyngham has told you the significance of such a snake.'

'I thought you promised not to mention him until we got home.'

'Just a reference *en passant*. What has he told you of the yellow snakes of Epidaurus?'

'Nothing,' said Marius reluctantly.

'They are the sacred serpents of the Temple of Asclepius. They heal the sick, by licking them in their sleep. You will find an account by Walter Pater in *Marius the Epicurean*, the imaginary biography, largely confined to religious activities, of a young Roman namesake of yours. He came here – or to some similar shrine of Asclepius – for a cure.'

'What had he got?' Marius enquired.

'Acute discontent, common then as now among the rich and idle. This place and those like it were the ancient equivalent of Aix-les-Bains or Baden-Baden. One came here for rest and peace of mind. Mind you, there were the same kinds of injurious distractions – gambling and luxurious restaurants. But if you could resist these and surrender to the beauty of the countryside you had some sort of a chance.'

They walked away from the theatre, along a track which took them past the low-built museum, then turned right over a stream and towards the excavations.

'Did Marius find peace of mind here?' Marius asked.

'For a time.'

'And then?'

'I rather think he became a Christian. His spiritual progress, as told in Pater's ponderous prose, is a great trial of one's patience. So you will forgive me if I cannot be too precise about its later stages. But I do recall quite clearly that Marius was kissed or licked by a yellow serpent of Asclepius, and was thus rendered temporarily stable, at about the half-way mark of a longish book.'

'How did Marius end up?'

'As I told you, I don't remember the details. But one thing I can tell you: after being licked by the yellow serpents, he strove consciously and constantly for virtue.'

'Is that a hint? Now I've seen one of them, am I supposed to strive too?'

'I saw it as well. Perhaps both of us should begin striving.'

'The trouble is,' said Marius as they came to a temple, 'virtue is so beastly boring and unattractive.'

'It is easier on the nerves and the constitution – as your eponym discovered – than the pursuit of pleasure.'

'That's old men's talk. This is the Temple of Asclepius?'

'No. There's nothing left of that. This is the Temple of Themis, who personifies Justice. The day is crammed with moral lessons.'

'A few weeks ago,' said Marius, 'when I was travelling through Italy with Piero Caspar before we met you in Brindisi, Piero was laying on the moral lessons as well. It seems that I am considered a natural target for them.'

'We all desire to improve you,' Jeremy said.

'You know,' said Marius, 'that I was coming through Italy to betray you? To turn you back home before you could find what you were looking for. I was too late. When Piero and I reached Brindisi, you had already . . . already found your Grail, so to speak.'

'Why should you have wished me not to?'

'I was being tested . . . to make sure of my obedience, I believe, though other motives were alleged. But what it comes down to is that my loyalty was being tried by Raisley Conyngham.'

'I thought,' said Jeremy, 'that we were not allowed to mention him.'

'You are not. I am when I wish, as I cannot explain myself or my behaviour without reference to him. I have to explain myself now, Jeremy. You had been sent out by Theodosia and Carmilla to redeem yourself after your disgrace in Australia. Right?'

'Right.'

'You were to sail westward from Ithaca, with Fielding for company, until you came to the "Islands of the Blessèd", a figure of speech that intimated some vision or marvel which you would recognize as the sign of redemption, granted after your long endeavour, and as the conclusion of your search. Raisley Conyngham commanded me to stop all this, since it was not what he wished, and have you brought home. First I begged Carmilla to recall you, but she would not. Yet I obtained permission from her to go and try you in person, provided that Piero came with me as a kind of umpire and duenna. We had news of you as you approached Brindisi, but by the time we got there you had met with your marvel and your journey was done, so that I was too late to do anything about it myself.'

'Which brings us to the question,' said Jeremy, 'of what you would have done if you had found me before I had had my . . . vision. Were you still minded, after your journey through Italy with Piero, to betray me by denying me my passage to the "Islands of the Blessèd"?'

'I was just coming to that. But first . . . tell me, Jeremy: what was it you saw which made you realize that your search was over? That you were redeemed?'

'I saw myself as the friend and confidant of the poet Virgil. I spoke to him as he died, there in Brindisi nearly 2,000 years ago, and comforted him, and saved him from traitors who were trying to steal his poetry from him.'

'That is to say, Jeremy, that you somehow imagined all this?'

'No. It happened. To say "I saw myself" as Virgil's friend is wrong. I was his friend. I was part of his being and he was part of mine.'

'And that is what I might have taken from you if I had come upon you earlier and persuaded you to go home?'

'Yes. So I must know, Marius, here in the Temple of Themis who is Justice, would you have taken this from me had you been able?'

'I should not have known what I was taking. How could I have known?'

'Granted. But would you deliberately have tried to take from me whatever God or miracle or Cup or portent might come to me and redeem me?'

'How can I know?'

'You set out to do it.'

'I might have changed my mind.'

'And displeased Raisley Conyngham?'

21

Marius scowled. 'I told you: I am the one who will talk of Raisley Conyngham, when I wish.'

'We can hardly conduct this discussion without my being allowed to as well.'

'Yes, we can,' snapped Marius. 'You must simply conceive that I act as I see fit. Whatever is suggested to me by anyone else, I do my will.'

'Yet you are so uncertain of yourself that you do not know what this would have been?'

'No. But I should have known when I saw you.'

'How?'

'I should have been told.'

'By whom?'

'My *daimon*. My genius. The god who guides me.'

'Your conscience?'

'No. My personal *daimon* who watches over me. We all have one. Raisley Conyngham wants power over mine. He has some – not yet enough for him, and much less when I am far away from him – from his charm and his persuasion. He still has too little, Jeremy, to have forced my *daimon* to force me to betray you. Had I done so, it would have been more from jealousy than out of desire to please Mr Conyngham. Though that desire was real enough, it would not have been strong enough, by itself, to move me or my *daimon*, without the jealousy I felt because I wanted you at home with me, not sailing the ocean with Fielding Gray at the behest of those two women.'

'Jealousy is the meanest vice of all. If your *daimon* could not rid you of it, then he were a poor *daimon* indeed – more under Raisley Conyngham's influence than you might think.'

'Only *I* am to talk of Raisley Conyngham.'

Marius was verging on a tantrum.

'Come on,' said Jeremy. 'Time to go back to Nauplion. Let us talk no more of this.'

Marius trembled. 'First . . . I must see another yellow serpent,' he said.

'They do not come,' said Jeremy, 'just for the asking. Not even to pretty boys like you.'

'Then I shall remember that one we saw on the theatre floor . . . which went gliding away into the forest. My *daimon* tells me to remember it.'

Gradually Marius grew calmer.

'The personal *daimon* or genius,' said Jeremy, as they walked back towards the stream, 'is a Platonic concept put in the mouth of Socrates, in *The Apology* and elsewhere. Who introduced you to the concept?'

'I did,' said Marius. 'I was to read *The Apology* with Raisley Conyngham during one holiday. But we only read the end of it, the only part worth reading, he said, where Socrates conjectures what death may hold for him. But I thought it would be worth while to go back and look at the rest. So later, some time later . . . last summer, when I was staying with Auntie Flo in Burnham . . . I did. And then I realized for the first time that, as Socrates premises of himself and of all men, I had my own *daimon* or *daimonion*: my own particle, perhaps, of God.'

The tide rose and made an island of Sandy Lodge for three nights. On the fourth it came high enough to flood Auntie Flo's ground floor to a depth of six inches. Upstairs Theodosia lay in labour, while Auntie Flo, ably attended by Carmilla, played the midwife. Despite the difficulties that had plagued the conception, there were none about the birth. It was a straightforward affair of pain and blood that cost Theodosia a groaning but no extreme trauma. The infant female, once ejected, was

23

promptly seized by its heels and started up by a no-nonsense slap from Auntie Flo. It then wailed fit to drown the wind, was washed, bedded and named.

'May as well get that straight,' said Auntie Flo, 'before Canteloupe comes blundering along. We'll have to let him know – if the telephone's still working. And when he gets here he'll want to choose the name himself. You know how overbearing men are.'

'Keep him away from here,' said Theodosia. 'Tell him I'll bring the child back when I'm ready, and meanwhile that it's got everything it should have and nothing extra. We've both known it would be a girl since the test was made late last summer, and I decided long ago that it should be called Nausikaa.* Marius will like that and he deserves some say in the matter.'

'Nausikaa it shall be,' said Carmilla: 'a princess of the Phaeacians.'

'Now get some rest, girl,' said Auntie Flo.

As Carmilla and Auntie Flo drank Marc de Bourgogne in Auntie Flo's bedroom, Carmilla said to her hostess:

'Unless there is a boy later on, that child will be called Baroness Sarum of Old Sarum when Canteloupe dies. The Barony descends in the female line.'

'Not the Marquessate?'

'No. There was originally a complicated special remainder for heirs male of the first Marquis's eldest daughter – that's how Canty got the thing. But none of that entitles Canty's daughter to inherit anything other than the Barony and the property.'

'Which should be enough to be going on with,' said Auntie Flo. 'But if Canteloupe dies without a male heir, the Marquessate is done for?'

---

* Correctly spelt and pronounced in four syllables, Naūsīkăā, but commonly shortened in speech to Naūsīkă

'Right,' said Carmilla.

'Pity.'

'Do you really think so?'

'What will the girl be called now, while Canteloupe lives?'

'Lady Nausikaa Sarum,' said Carmilla: 'what else?'

'As daughter of a Marquess,' said Auntie Flo, 'she will take precedence as a Countess. But if she actually inherits the Barony on Canteloupe's decease, what precedence will she take then? Still as a Countess?'

'A nice conundrum,' said Carmilla. 'When I telephone Canty, I'll ask him. He'll know.'

'Not very tactful to refer to what will happen when he's dead.'

'He won't mind that. There's a lot of things to be said against Canteloupe,' Carmilla said: 'that he's arrogant, deceitful and callous; but one thing is also very clear; that he's far too grand to be piqued by the idea of death.'

'Here is your daughter,' said Theodosia Canteloupe to Marius Stern: 'Lady Nausikaa Sarum.'

Marius and Jeremy bent to examine the uncovered sex of the sleeping child, and then the rest of it.

'She favours Teresa Malcolm,' said Marius. 'Teresa – Tessa – has been with you to comfort you, when she was not at school, all the time you have been carrying this child. Why is she not here now?'

'Her aunt, Mrs Malcolm, is ill. Teresa is with her in London.'

'Mrs Malcolm must be very ill indeed for Tessa to desert you at such a time.'

'She is very ill,' said Theodosia.

'Fielding Gray is with her too,' said Carmilla.

'And my sister, Rosie?'

'She is in the Languedoc with your mother. But Teresa

25

has the two Blessington girls to support her, Jakki and Carolyn. And of course their father.'

'I do not understand,' said Marius. 'Mrs Malcolm is never ill.'

'She is now,' Carmilla said.

'I should go to her,' said Marius. 'What is she ill with?'

'*Anno domini*,' Carmilla said.

'She is not all that old.'

'Some bodies wear out quicker than others,' said Theodosia.

'In any case, I should go to her,' Marius repeated. 'We have not always agreed, Mrs Malcolm and I . . . but for a long time she has been there for me. And I for her, I think.'

'She wants nobody,' said Carmilla; 'nobody except Fielding and Teresa.'

'You said Jakki and Carolyn – '

' – They help Teresa by being kind to her when she is not with her aunt. They do not see Mrs Malcolm.'

'But she always liked them very much.'

'She will not see them now,' Carmilla said. 'I have had full accounts from their father, Ivan Blessington. And from Fielding. Maisie will see nobody except Fielding himself, her niece, Teresa, and her doctor, Doctor La Soeur.'

'I thought he'd retired,' said Auntie Flo.

'So he has. He is attending Maisie Malcolm,' said Carmilla, 'by special request. So you stay put here, young Marius. I'll drive you back to school on the fifteenth, on my way back to Cambridge.'

The next day, 11 January, Theodosia Canteloupe was to take Nausikaa home to her official father, the Marquess Canteloupe, in his great house in Wiltshire. Jeremy was leaving too; for now that his holiday with Marius was done he must return, he said, to his estate at Luffham-by-Whereham.

'Why?' grizzled Marius. 'You told me the estate runs itself.'

'What with one thing and another, *caro*, I have been away, apart from odd days at Christmas, for a very long time. I must now, so to speak, sit on my throne for a while. And then, Marius (*dimidia pars mei*), my father is there and an old servant who likes to see me. You will be all right here with Auntie Florence . . . and Carmilla.'

Before Jeremy left, he went on a long drive with Carmilla. Marius, who wanted to accompany them, was told firmly by Auntie Florence that he must stay with Theodosia and their daughter.

'You have just had two weeks of pure pleasure,' Auntie Flo said; 'now you can think of other people and show a little civility.'

The disgruntled Marius was not very pleasant to Theodosia. The baby partly bored and partly frightened him – that such a creature (he thought) should have sprung from his throbbing prick. With Theodosia he had little to discuss. All he could think of was the castles and temples of the Peloponnese in the grey light of January, as he drove with Jeremy by the shore of the misty sea. Now that was over, and he was soon to return to school for the dullest Quarter of the year (having been on leave of absence ever since the previous autumn), and if all that was not enough, Jeremy and Carmilla had deserted him, had left him flat to talk to this dismal woman with the child that reminded him of Teresa . . . Teresa who was at the sick bed of a woman who never before had been sick.

'Try not to look so bored and sulky,' said Theodosia; 'you showed me kindness and love in the spring.'

'And then you threw me out of the house for my pains.

27

Because I succeeded in exciting you, and you felt that was beneath your dignity, you threw me out like a dog.'

'You made me forget myself – or very nearly. I hated you for that. But not any more.'

'Shall you want me to come to you again, if Canteloupe asks you to try for a boy?'

'I cannot tell what is to happen about that.'

'I shan't much want to come, you know, even if I am the one chosen.'

'You are the only one I could bear. Not so much for yourself, as for your friend, Galahad.'

'My dear friend, Galahad. God, how depressing you are. Why can't you be like your sister? Carmilla is *fun* to be with in bed. Carmilla takes a delight in it all. You fight against it. Carmilla *comes*. You sort of . . . dry up instead. And then you pitch a chap out of the house . . . without any dinner.'

'Perhaps I deserve this, Marius. But show kindness again.'

Marius, shamed, made an effort.

'I wonder what is the matter with Mrs Malcolm? Surely Teresa has told you. Surely she has telephoned or written to you.'

'Teresa has told me nothing about Mrs Malcolm. I do not think that she wishes to talk of her, even to write of her, to me.'

'Yes. I think I can understand that. And yet you and Teresa love each other, Thea. Tessa has . . . borne this child of ours together with you. And now this illness of Mrs Malcolm's is keeping you apart. Surely Teresa has told you what is the matter with her aunt, or at least how long it is likely to go on?'

'Teresa has told me nothing.'

'In a very few days she will be back at school with me

28

on Farncombe Hill. Then you will not see her until the first Absit of the Quarter.'

'I know. But Teresa owes everything to her Auntie Maisie, who has been a mother to her. Of course she must be with her now.'

'But *what* can the matter be with her?'

Theodosia shrugged. 'It is time to feed Nausikaa,' she said.

'Go ahead. I don't mind.'

'I'm afraid I do, Marius,' said Theodosia, shrinking slightly. 'Go away, please.'

'God knows why I was made to stay in the house,' said Marius, and went off to be disagreeable to Auntie Florence.

At about the same time as Theodosia offered her breast to Nausikaa, Carmilla said to Jeremy:

'Marius was badly miffed at being left behind. But I have some questions.'

'Ask that it may be answered.'

The Bristol Channel gleamed briefly beyond and below the brown bracken to the right of the road. Then the road turned and they were walled in, on both sides, by tall silent conifers.

'How did you find Marius in Greece?' Carmilla said.

'Enchanting. And grateful.'

'Did he talk of Brindisi?'

'He told me he came there to betray me, but he was not sure whether he would have done. Had he arrived in time, he might, or might not, have changed his mind.'

'And where was Raisley Conyngham in all this?'

'Marius was anxious not to talk of Raisley – except strictly on his own terms. He obviously wants to please Raisley, but he insists that he is independent of him. In the end he obeys, he says, his own *daimon*.'

'Good.'

'Not so good. He admitted that he felt jealous because I was away with Fielding. I said that jealousy was the meanest of all emotions and that his *daimon* could not be healthy if it permitted him to harbour it. I suggested that his *daimon* could have been tainted by Raisley's influence.'

'His reaction?'

'Neurotic anger. It was the only time we nearly had a scene. He managed to control himself, but only just.'

'You know,' said Carmilla, 'we shall never quite know what we are up against until we have a complete understanding of Raisley Conyngham.'

'Never mind a complete understanding,' said Jeremy. 'We must simply get rid of him. We understand enough, we have seen enough, to know that.'

'So we have all been saying for some time. But how? We must know something that we can use, either to vanquish him or disgrace him. We must make detailed investigation instead of indulging in casual speculation. We must get a team together, do our research and reconnaissance, then work out an exact yet malleable plan and put it into disciplined action.'

'Very well,' said Jeremy; 'let there be a team. Although I must be at Luffham quite a lot these coming weeks, I should be glad if I might be included.'

'Oh yes. You and I are Founder Members.'

'Whom else shall we co-opt?'

'You will let me decide?'

'Happily.'

'Then I shall summon you within ten days to meet them.'

While Carmilla was driving Marius through Salisbury on their way between Burnham-on-Sea and Guildford (for Farncombe), Marius said, 'Pity that house of Flo's is so poky. I was longing for you while we were there. It's been quite a time, Carmilla.'

'Yes,' she said. 'I'm not sure I trust you any more, if ever I did. Why did you raise all that row about Jeremy's journey in the autumn? Why did you try to spoil it?'

'I spoiled nothing.'

'Only because you came up with Jeremy too late,' Carmilla said.

'As I have already told Jeremy, I might have done nothing – even if I had been in time.'

'Might. What made you think that you had to interfere at all?'

'You know very well. You know who has my ear; you all do. You keep complaining about him and trying to crab him and saying what a rotten influence he is – not straight out to my face or his, but slyly, like old maids behind lace curtains.'

'You are so beautiful, Marius. No one likes to offend you openly.'

'What has he ever done except teach me the classics and how to behave in the world at large?'

'He tried to make you kill little Tully Sarum last summer,' said Carmilla; 'and so you would have done had you not been interrupted by the accident which killed him instead. He tried to make you betray Jeremy – and in so doing to betray Theodosia and me by spoiling our plans for his journey.'

'In both cases, there were reasons. A lot depends on one's point of view.'

'You are too young to play the sophist. Even if you were older, the part would not become you. It becomes nobody.'

'Anyway,' said Marius gently, 'none of this can be proved.'

31

'Don't be disingenuous, Marius. Lack of proof does not mean lack of blame.'

'Legally and officially it does.'

Carmilla stopped the car by a seedy pub.

'Get out,' she said.

A few yards up the street from the pub was the East Gate into the Cathedral Close (as opposed to the Main Gate, at the south-west corner, near the second-hand bookshop). Carmilla and Marius walked along a road with fine, rich, peaceful houses to left and to right, and then, when the houses on the left ceased, veered left on to the Cathedral Green and made for the West Portal of the building.

'Why are we coming here?' Marius said.

'Don't you like it?'

'I like it very much. Can we do what you and Jeremy did in Bishop Alcocke's Chantry in the cathedral at Ely?'

'Who told you that tale?'

'You did.'

'I don't think there is anywhere suitable in this one. Anyway, we shan't have time. We have come to look at something special. There is a tomb, and on it the effigy of an unknown knight. Fielding Gray told me about it once. He said the knight's face closely resembled that of a boy with whom he had been in love, many years ago, at your school.'*

'Why do you wish to see this?' Marius asked.

'Fielding said that the knight on the tomb, like the boy he loved at school, was a type of pure innocence. Yet the boy was later driven to kill himself by the suspicion and spite of people who should have known better.'

Carmilla took Marius by the right wrist. She led him up the south side aisle, turned right, then left behind a

* See *Fielding Gray* by S. R. (Blond & Briggs, 1967)

wooden screen and into a deep shadow. Surely Salisbury Cathedral was all light? she thought. Surely Fielding hadn't warned her about this shadow? Too late to bother about that now. She must have followed Fielding's directions correctly, because discernible despite the shadow was a tomb, and on the tomb a stone figure in chain armour, legs straight, prayerful fingers pointing up to a mailed chin, the face of a stripling, almost a child.

'I can hardly see him in this light,' Marius said.

'Oh, but I can. I have the sharp eyes of a scholar for this kind of work. He had a full mouth, turned very slightly downwards at the corners, a soft nose, mild, beseeching eyes. The face of innocence. Not at all like your face,' Carmilla said, 'which is what I came here to establish. It was my last hope, you see, that I might be mistaken, that we all might be mistaken, and that I might find, in this face of innocence, at least some of the same traits as I find in yours . . . which would mean that your spirit had not been wholly cankered. But while this mouth is still uncertain and ready to give thanks or ask mercy, yours is firm and decided, almost scornful. While these eyes hope for love, yours demand submission. You have been told by one in whom you believe that "Do what thou wilt shall be the whole of the law", provided that what "thou wilt" is also what he wills for you . . . however monstrous, however profane.'

'I don't know about being told. My *daimon* is still my own.'

'Is it, Marius? I think the Devil is in it. Or at least that innocence is for ever out of it.'

'Thank you,' said Marius, 'for the concession. Listen, Carmilla,' he said, moving close up behind her; 'have you ever read a French book called *Montaillou*? It has recently been translated into English.'

'The book about the Cathars?'

'Yes. Raisley Conyngham recommended it to me. You will recall that the Cathars or Albigensians believed that the Devil, acting as Demiurge, had made this world with its lusts and vanities.' He pressed still closer behind her, till she was up against the ledge of the slab on which lay the young knight. 'To be saved,' Marius went on, 'one must forswear these lusts and vanities; but one was allowed to postpone that until one was on one's death bed, so that one might enjoy a life of pleasure right up to a few hours before death. Later on,' said Marius, stroking her strong belly, 'the Cathars began to believe that the Demiurge or Devil was in no way beneath God, in no way depending on his sufferance or inferior to him in might; they began to believe that there were in fact two Gods, equal and co-eternal, one of whom created and shaped the flesh and the other the spirit; and that now a man must choose between them – not abandon himself to one for life and seek sanctuary with the other by repenting just before death, but decide which God would ultimately be victorious in the struggle between the pair of them, on pain of being damned if he chose the wrong one. You understand, Carmilla? Though I think that you, the scholar, should be explaining all this to me, rather than the other way about.'

'Your exegesis is very clear, Marius. And, I think, more or less correct. It does not follow that the doctrines of the Cathars or Albigensians are true.'

'But you would agree,' said Marius, rubbing himself gently against her trousered buttocks and continuing to massage her belly, 'that if their later doctrines are true, if God and the Devil (or Demiurge) are in fact equal and co-eternal, and if they are in fact struggling with each other to decide which of them will ultimately rule the universe, then it is necessary to choose one side or the other . . . if one hopes to find salvation as the faithful servant of the final victor. I think you are going to come, Carmilla?'

'Perhaps. Not just yet.'

'Well then. Let us say, by way of variation, that God and the Devil are not struggling any longer and have agreed on a truce, a perpetual truce. Since both are rational, this would probably be the most sensible solution. In that case, Carmilla, one does not have to wager which will be the eventual victor but simply to decide which deity one finds the more congenial. One can even change sides, as neither deity is any longer prepared to fight for adherents or to punish disloyalty. So, Carmilla: my personal and independent *daimon*, which has a spark of both deities in it, can vacillate for as long and as often as it wishes; and to say that it is impaired, or cankered, or corrupt, or even to say that innocence has left it, is absolute nonsense – in a universe, Carmilla, in which God and the Devil have agreed to differ in tranquillity. You are going to come, Carmilla.'

'Even if the deities are equal,' quavered Carmilla, 'and have sworn a truce, one is still Good and the other Evil.'

'But in practical terms, in terms of damnation or salvation, it makes no difference. Neither deity can punish the followers of the other.'

'There must be conscience,' squealed Carmilla; and then, although she usually came rather gently, she jerked and heaved against the tombstone of the innocent knight, while Marius sighed and shuddered behind her.

As soon as Carmilla had dropped Marius at his school at the top of Farncombe Hill, he went to the Domus Vestalis (Vestal or Virginal House) of which Teresa Malcolm was a member. He waited politely in the Locker Hall while a *famula* (female duty fag) went to fetch Miss Malcolm.

'Very efficient, your Domus,' said Marius to Tessa as they walked on the terrace over the cricket green, 'having a *famula* posted on the first afternoon of the Quarter.'

'She was briefed on the last day of last Quarter,' said Tessa, holding one wing of her gold-auburn hair against the January wind which blew up from the valley. 'These things are very easy to get right if only you think a little ahead.'

She said nothing more. Although she had joined him on the walk without demur (New Year Spirit, he thought) she was clearly leaving the effort of initiating a topic to Marius, which, on the whole, suited him very well. The dusk was settling and he must be direct.

'Tessa,' he said, 'what is the matter with your aunt, Mrs Malcolm? Why could you not be present when Thea's child was born?'

'I did not like to remember that it was yours. I could not bear that you had done her violence to get it.'

'I did her no violence. She herself will tell you how gentle I was.'

'To do . . . what you did . . . at all was a violence to Theodosia.'

'She willed it, she invited me to do it . . . and I had to put up with some very unkind and captious behaviour when it was done. And well done, as it turned out.'

'She was unpleasant to you because you had violated her. You should not have done that, Marius, even if she did invite you. You should have known that she consented only because Canteloupe commanded.'

'Men to blame, I see, as usual. Let's drop that, Tessa. What I want to know is this: you have spent every moment you could, for many months now, comforting and caring for Theodosia in her pregnancy; and yet when it came to the climax, you were not there.'

'She needed a good nurse, not me.'

36

'She might have needed your love. You were not there, I was told, because your aunt was dangerously ill. Never in my life have I known a stronger or healthier woman than your Auntie Maisie; and then she was suddenly so ill that you could not leave her to come to Somerset?'

'She was.'

'And still is?'

'She is better. Otherwise I should not be here. Doctor La Soeur has found a drug for her.'

'When did her illness start?'

'I was called from Canteloupe's house in Wiltshire on New Year's Day.'

'And what did you find in London?'

'I found my Auntie Maisie lying in bed and refusing to move or talk. Refusing to move or talk *at all*, Marius.'

'Jesus Christ.'

'That's what I thought. Nursing her was . . . very trying. Luckily Fielding Gray had come with me to help.'

'And you both called in Doctor La Soeur . . . although he has retired?'

'No true doctor ever retires.'

'What did Doctor La Soeur say the matter was?' Marius pressed on.

'Withdrawal.'

'That was obvious. What had caused it?'

'He thought . . . that she had some secret; that she was so scared of revealing this and yet was under such emotional pressure to do so that the only way of keeping it to herself was to cease to communicate altogether.'

'Under what emotional pressure?'

'I am not quite sure. Doctor La Soeur said that she yearned, that was his word, yearned to reveal her secret – and yet was terrified of the possible result. I think . . . that Fielding may know what the secret is. But he has refused to say anything about it.'

37

'And now . . . she is herself again?'

'No,' said Tessa. 'She behaves more or less normally and she addresses people on day to day matters. She gives orders to the hotel staff at Buttock's; she realized when I must return to school and sent a servant to get a ticket for me. But she is not herself, Marius. There is no zest. Always before . . . she has treated the smallest things with interest and gaiety. No longer. She didn't even come to watch me pack. She used to be so helpful, and so funny, that I forgot to be sad that I was leaving her. This time . . . I was there alone, crying into my trunk.'

'You have left her often enough this last half year,' said Marius, 'without too much sadness.'

'To be with Theodosia. I had to go to her.'

'I dare say. But your aunt will have noticed, she must have noticed, how eager you always were to get away. She was alone at Christmas. Perhaps this made her feel deserted and unhinged her mind.'

'How can you be so cruel, Marius? I've told you, Doctor La Soeur said she had some secret – '

'Could that secret have been her own loneliness and despair?'

Tessa turned and walked away along the dark terrace with the wind behind her, staggering from time to time as it nearly laid her on her face.

Marius next went to the private Lodgings of his tutor, Raisley Conyngham, where he told his master, in a somewhat troubled fashion, of his talk with Tessa.

'Why did you upset her like that?' Raisley Conyngham said.

'She deserves it. She has been altogether too smug ever since Thea Canteloupe took her up. But she must not be distressed for long. Later on, sir, I shall persuade Major Gray to tell me what the secret really is, and then tell

38

Tessa, so that she will know that it is not her absences in Wiltshire that have caused her aunt's illness.'

'How do you know it isn't?'

'Because Mrs Malcolm has always said she didn't mind, that she is glad Tessa is going to such a grand house to learn about the world with such distinguished people.'

'Mrs Malcolm could be lying about that. But as it happens she isn't – at least I very much doubt it. If my guess is right,' Raisley Conyngham said, 'the secret which she suddenly finds uncontainable yet unrevealable is that she was for many years a very successful and very versatile whore.'

'SIR?'

'A whore, boy. You know what that is. She gave rather special exhibitions. I went to one of them once, an anonymous member of the audience. We all wore masks, you see, in the Venetian manner. She threw them in with the tickets – as well she might have done considering her exorbitant charge.'

'I don't think I can tell Tessa that this is her aunt's secret.'

'I dare say not,' said Raisley Conyngham: 'so she will continue to think that your suggestion may be true that Mrs Malcolm is pining to despair because Teresa herself is so often away from her.'

'That Tessa should think that for long would be intolerable,' Marius said. 'A brief punishment was all I wished to inflict. Not permanent misery.'

'Then you should not have suggested what you did.'

'How can I set this right, sir? I shan't be happy until I have done so.'

Raisley Conyngham rang for his housekeeper and ordered tea and crumpets, though it was already nearly six o'clock.

'You have had a long journey,' he said, 'and no luncheon, to judge from the look of you.'

'We went to Salisbury Cathedral instead.'

'Good. You must be familiar with all the great cathedrals. It is expected of one. Now, as to this matter of Teresa. I shall show you how to set it right – not for her sake, but because her distress so obviously distresses you.'

'Thank you, sir.'

'But this is a weakness in you, and I shall have to punish as well as relieve you. I don't want this sort of soppiness to occur again. Meanwhile, the thing is quite simple. You may use my telephone to ring up Fielding Gray, who, Teresa told you, is at Buttock's tending her aunt. He most certainly knows the secret which we have just been discussing, but it is my belief that he knows another as well – one more suitable to tell to Teresa, let us hope. He is, after all, Mrs Malcolm's most intimate friend in all the world.'

'And the punishment you have in store for me, sir?'

'As to that, you will soon see. Now, in order to console Teresa, you must first extract this second secret I refer to from Fielding Gray, and you will need a key to unlock him. So: tell him that unless he tells you a new and more acceptable secret (for you know he possesses one) that could account for Mrs Malcolm's mental trauma, you will be compelled, for want of another, to tell Teresa the one you *have* discovered, i.e. Mrs Malcolm's career as a strumpet. Anything, you will say, rather than have Teresa continue so stricken by your own suggestion that her aunt's illness has been caused by her own, Teresa's, desertion.'

'But I couldn't – '

' – Couldn't is not a word in my vocabulary, boy. Couldn't what, for the Lord's sake?'

By the Lord, thought Marius, he does not mean Christ or the Christian God. Just now (though not always) I wish he did.

'I couldn't tell Tessa her aunt is bursting to confess to having been a harlot; and I couldn't blackmail Fielding Gray by threatening to do so.'

'You can certainly take the latter course. That is your punishment,' said Raisley Conyngham: 'to be compelled to do something you find abhorrent in order to rectify something you find even more abhorrent. It will be good training for you, an important lesson well learned. The practice may come in useful later on. Furthermore, from now on you may be more careful to see to it that you do not get into such silly and injurious predicaments. All ways round, I shall be well pleased for you to receive such disagreeable instruction.'

So Marius rang up Fielding Gray at Buttock's Hotel, where he was staying in the room that was permanently kept for him (as part owner) by Maisie Malcolm, who owned the other part and managed the place. Marius knew and asked for the correct number of the extension to Fielding's room, but for some reason he was put through to Mrs Malcolm's. It was quite possible, Marius reflected, that Mrs Malcolm had given special instructions to the switchboard that this should happen; for Maisie was a woman of insatiable curiosity, and it might well be more than she could bear (even if she was not yet quite up to snuff) that telephone calls should get through to Fielding Gray and she not know of them.

'Marius Stern,' said Marius. 'I'm sorry you've been ill, Mrs Malcolm.'

'That's very civil of you to say so, young Marius, but I can't think that's what you telephoned for.'

Marius did a little fast thinking. Obviously he was never

going to get through to Fielding Gray now without a long inquisition from Maisie. But he ought to be able to use Maisie to find matter for consoling Tessa, in which case he could postpone telephoning Fielding, or perhaps would not need to telephone him at all (thus saving himself from Raisley Conynham's 'punishment').

'The thing is, Mrs Malcolm,' Marius said, 'that Tessa is very upset about something and I'm trying to cheer her up.'

'You leave Tessa alone.'

'I don't mean her any harm, Mrs Malcolm. We're old friends, when all is said. And speaking to her as an old friend this evening, I found out that she is very depressed by the idea that she might be to blame for your illness.'

'How could she be?'

'Perhaps . . . by being away so much. Perhaps you missed her more than either of you realized. Anyway, that's what she's come to think, and she's very miserable. I wondered whether . . . whether you might be able to tell me something that might reassure her.'

For a few seconds there was silence.

'Mrs Malcolm? Are you there?'

'I'm here, boy. Let's get a few things straight. You know what form my illness took?'

'You . . . you withdrew.'

'You might call it that.' Suddenly Maisie's voice changed from a dreary and monotonous mumble to something taut and plangent, like the plucked string of a lute. 'But it wasn't because Tessa was away – I was glad for her to be away with Lady Canteloupe and the rest, do you hear, glad.' The lute quickened and began to twang. 'It's just that there's something she ought to know and ought not to know. Why am I telling you? Because perhaps you'll help her more and not cut her dead at one minute and get horny over her the next.'

'I don't get horny over her.' Marius remembered hearing from Fielding Gray that Maisie was subject to importunate fantasies about the lusts which she imagined men brewed up for her niece. 'And it's her that cuts me.'

'With good reason – if she thinks you want to mess her up.'

'I've told you. I don't want to mess her – '

'I've heard that story before, not just from you. Anyway, I'm going to tell you something that'll stop you.'

Surely not the first secret of which Raisley had spoken, that Maisie had been a bawd? Why should that stop his wanting to 'mess Tessa up', always assuming he did want to?

'It had better stop you,' Maisie twanged. 'Otherwise I'll slit you. Slit you. Do you understand what I'm saying?'

'Mrs Malcolm. I only want to help Tessa to understand that your illness had nothing to do with her, or her visits to Lady Canteloupe.'

'Nothing to do with her and Lady Canteloupe, no. I've told you already. Anything that keeps Tessa away from men is all right with me. Mind you, I let Fielding see her again now, I used not to because they fancied each other – '

' – Mrs Malcolm – '

' – But ever since she's been going with Lady Canteloupe I know she's all right. So I don't mind how long or often she's away in that gallery, oh dear no.' The pace of the lute quickened, the note grew shriller. 'But I'll tell you a thing. Though Tessa wasn't to blame for my illness, she was a sort of cause of it. A catalyst, don't they call it? I can't bear it, Marius. I must tell her yet I mustn't, so I decide to shut right up altogether. But then La Soeur brings me round again. He gives me dope, so that I can be a person again but still stay shut up, sealed up, because I tell him that I must. But I hate dope, Marius, so I chucked it all away, and the seal has gone, Marius, the

43

seal is broken, Marius, and you're the first that's spoken to me since and I can't stop myself and here's what I'm telling you to tell my Tessa though whether or not it'll stop her being miserable, God alone knows, but it'll make you keep your hot grubby hands off her honeypot, or if it doesn't I'll slit you. She's mine, Marius, all mine. My child, my child, my daughter. And do you know who got up my quim to get her? *Your dad*, years ago, when he came to me one night while your ma was trying to have a baby, one of them what died, before she had beautiful you at last, which was not all that long after, come to think of it, perhaps your daddy was turning lucky, anyway he certainly put a bimbo in my belly. You know how? You know why? Because I was so sad when your daddy telephoned the hospital, and we heard that the baby was dead, dead in the hospital, they didn't know why, not them – I was so sad, I was so desperate for him, that I let him do it, made him do it without either of us wearing anything, just to see what happened, to see what God got up to next. And what happened was Tessa, that's what God got up to making next, God spurting out of your daddy's dainty prick – circumcised I remember, I remember to this day, with a little scar where the Rabbi had nicked him, he said, yes *he* said, pretty Marius, *your daddy*, what shot his lovely load up my twotty-pie and by the Grace of God almighty made my daughter, your half-sister, Tessa, Teresa, your half-sister and my baby-pooh. Sorry dear,' she said, suddenly dull and dreary again. 'I get carried away, you see, whenever I think of that night with your dad, Gregory. Gregory the Jew; gentleman Gregory that rode with the King's Guard; Gregory, the father of my Tessa.'

'Why couldn't you have told her, told her long ago?'

'Because I was a tart and had her off a client. No matter it was your dad, he was still a client. If Tessa knew she was my child and then found out that I was a whore, that her mother was a whore . . .'

'Yes. I understand. What shall I tell her, Maisie?'

'No respect, you see. No sooner you know I was a tart than you start calling me Maisie.'

'I'm sorry. It wasn't like that. You must know it wasn't. I wanted to show that I sympathize, that all this has made me fonder of you than I ever was before. But what shall I tell Tessa? Or what shall you tell her? She has to be told something before she eats her heart out thinking that you were made ill by her neglect.'

'Don't you touch her, don't you touch her lovely skin or I'll slit you,' Maisie howled down the telephone, and rang off.

'I can't tell Tessa any of this,' said Marius to Raisley Conyngham after summarizing his conversation with Maisie; 'do you suppose it's true?'

'We know she was a whore. Whether or not she was really Teresa's mother, by your father, we don't know. It's possible. Anything is possible in this sort of a circus. But you say the wretched woman is now mad?'

'She's thrown her drugs away. The ones prescribed by Doctor La Soeur. She started quite calmly, when she first answered, and then . . . fell apart. Then, when she'd finished the bit about conceiving Tessa, she was quite calm again – but not for long: she ended up screeching like crazy Cassandra.'

'Fielding Gray is staying there. He will deal with her, if anybody can,' Raisley Conyngham said.

'If she does go mad, Tessa will feel even worse about her. What shall I tell Tessa, sir?'

'What Mrs Malcolm told you. Or most of it.'

'But I can't, sir, I – '

'I told you there must be a punishment for your

45

feebleness. Now it will take a slightly different form. You must tell Teresa what her aunt – or her mother – told you. Then Teresa will know that the causes of Mrs Malcolm's illness were quite outside Teresa's control – that the illness was nothing to do with her absences but was caused by a longing that could not be gratified, Mrs Malcolm's longing to tell Teresa that she was her child.'

'And my half-sister? Got by my father?'

'I think,' said Raisley Conyngham, 'that is one part of the news which you might suppress. We don't, after all, know it to be true.'

'We don't know any of it to be true. Perhaps Mrs Malcolm's love for Tessa has caused the delusion that she bore her. And you surely don't expect me to tell Tessa that her mother was a whore?'

'Oh yes. An important part of your punishment. You can dress it up, of course . . . say that Mrs Malcolm was a discreet and high-class courtesan, as indeed she was. But you will definitely omit the exhibition which I attended. It was choice, Marius, very choice, but it might be rather crushing for a gently nurtured girl to hear about. And it would be very shocking for her to know your source of information – that is, me – on which she would no doubt insist. She is my pupil, when all is said.'

'So am I.'

'A different kind of pupil. A male pupil. And one with green eyes and blond hair, at that, a very curious combination, Marius, reminiscent of Lucifer, some might say. *You* can be told anything at all.'

'Thank you, sir. So. Tessa is to hear that she is not to blame for her aunt's illness, which was caused by a long inhibited yearning to tell Tessa that she is, in fact, her mother. She is also to hear that Mrs Malcolm was . . . let us say . . . an Aspasia. Only she is not to know that she was fathered by my father and that I am her half-brother.'

'It is always sensible to keep one's options open,' Raisley Conyngham said.

When Marius told Tessa that Maisie Malcolm was really her mother, Tessa laughed.

'I've guessed that for ages,' she said: 'what other explanation was there? Nothing much was ever said about the woman who was supposed to be my mother, and that little extremely unconvincing. So I realized, quite young, what "Auntie Maisie" must be up to and after a little longer I realized why. She must have done something appalling, I thought, and she didn't want me to know I was her child in case I got to know of whatever she had done and was violently ashamed of my own mother. After a little longer still, I worked out what she had done: occasional turns of phrase, little gestures that she hadn't meant to make but happened too quickly and naturally for her to suppress them, a few choice specimens of "Auntie Maisie's" gnomic wisdom – they all added up to "loose woman" and even to "tart".'

'To one so young? With no experience of such women?'

'A "hotel child", which was what I was, has very early experience of everything under the moon. There were a lot of tarts, superior and sometimes not so superior, in and out of Buttock's the whole time. "Auntie Maisie" never let on about them to me, but some of the servants did, particularly Giuliano, the third waiter, and I noticed how much their general style had in common with Auntie's.'

'Just what did Giuliano think he was up to?'

'He was an ally. He was commissariat (occasional choccy truffles) and also intelligence, giving me the low-down on the staff and the whole hotel. He got his kicks imparting worldly information in an innocent ear – lots of people do, I understand – and being an intelligent girl I was quite fascinated. But it wasn't Giuliano who drew the comparison between the tarts that used Buttock's and Auntie, it was me. An apt pupil.'

'Amen. So how long have you known all this?'

'Since about the time I came here, to this school. I love this school,' Tessa said, looking from the path on which they were walking down to the winding river and then up to the troops of fir trees on the slopes above them. 'I am very happy here. Why make a *thing* about Auntie Maisie's past? Why make a song and dance because she hadn't told me she was my mother? Go on with being happy, I said to myself: if she wants to tell me, she can. If not – well, she's keeping quiet because she loves me, so what's the matter with that?'

'What shall you do now that your mother has told me?'

'Nothing. Why should that make any difference? But it is a relief to know that my "auntie's" illness was caused by conflicting anxieties rather than by my neglect.'

'She's still very ill, Tessa. Unbalanced.'

'Not my fault,' said Tessa; 'her own. She made her own past, and this is the result of it.'

'A cool judgement.'

'Human misery is such,' said Tessa, 'that one has to make cool judgements in order to stay sane oneself. For instance, I believe some girls in my position would drive themselves crazy to know who their father was. Certainly, there's an adopted girl in my Domus who is doing that. For myself, I don't at all want to know who my father was, and it is at least possible that my mother couldn't tell me if I did. So why worry about that? The fact is that I am here, and well looked after, which is quite enough to be going on with. Only totally inadequate people worry about who their parents were, and they do it because they are too stupid or feeble to do anything else, they do it in order to excuse their failure of will and capacity in others' eyes and in their own.'

'How hard you are. Do you ever talk like this to Thea Canteloupe?'

'All the time. She mostly agrees with what I say. Thea is hard too. Except in her love for Canteloupe, and her love for me.'

The next day, Marius made another effort to reach Fielding Gray on the telephone. This time he was successful.

'Hang on, Fielding,' he said, 'while I put a lot of money in the box. We have things to talk about.'

Not wanting Raisley Conyngham to overhear this conversation, Marius was using the public box rather incongruously sited in Scholars' Cloister.

'You could have reversed the charges,' said Fielding when Marius had finished clanking florins down the slot.

'That would have made me feel inferior. Where is Mrs Malcolm? Last time I telephoned, she poached the call.'

'She poaches all calls,' Fielding said. 'But now she can't because she's had to be taken away. She was babbling to all and sundry about whoredoms and bastardies. Bad for the morale of the staff and offputting for the guests.'

'Taken away? To Bedlam, as it were?'

'Not quite that bad. To a discreet home that used to be run by Doctor La Soeur and has now been sold to a promising young colleague of his. Very disappointing, Maisie's behaviour. She has always been as solid as a brick, and this last summer she was as calm and contented as ever, reading books down at my place in Broughton Staithe. And now – ZAPP.'

'I suppose it had begun boiling up secretly. Under the surface.'

'Why should it have?' said Fielding crossly. 'The situation has been what it has been for many years. Why should she suddenly dissolve into pieces now?'

'There's really no point in enquiring,' said Marius. 'Does Tessa know yet?'

'I rang up the Head of her Domus, who made a silly fuss. So I told her to fetch Tessa, who didn't make a silly fuss.'

'Tess is very tough these days. "Things are what they are, and the results will be what they will be" – that's Tessa's message.'

'Then she's cribbed it from Dean Inge,' Fielding said.

'Those weren't her exact words. That was me cribbing from Dean Inge. What Tessa says is not quite so general in tone and expression. "The fact is that I am here," she said just now, "which is quite enough to be going on with." And now I am going on,' said Marius, 'to make a very helpful suggestion. Then I shall require information in return. All right?'

'I suppose so.'

'You'll need somebody to run Buttock's Hotel. We have a caretaker-cum-cook in our house in London – telephone number under "Stern, Mrs I." in the book. Nobody ever goes there and he has nothing to do. He is a brilliant cook and a very understanding and capable man. Give him a chance to manage Buttock's while Maisie's away. He answers to the name of Terpsichore.'

'What?'

'Terpsichore,' Marius said. 'He used to be happy with Ethel or Mavis, but he's been going steadily upmarket.'

'Well, I'll certainly talk to him. I think, Marius, that poor Maisie is going to be away for a long time,' said Fielding, and suddenly gave a little sob and then a much bigger one.

'Concentrate your mind,' said Marius, 'by answering

the questions I have for you, in return for my tip about Terpsichore. Now then. When Maisie answered my telephone call, which was intended for you, last night, she suddenly cracked and spilled the beans to me about being a naughty lady and being Tessa's mum. She also said that it was my father that begat Tessa.'

'How very Old Testament you sound.'

'My father was a Jew. Was it him . . . that begat Tessa? Or was Maisie making it up?'

'Maisie told me the whole story some time ago, when she was indubitably sane. I am as certain as a man can be that she was not making it up.'

'That's it then.'

'How much does Tessa know about *that*?'

'Tessa knows only that Mummy was a rorty girl and conceived Tessa in sin. Mummy never told her, but I did – and anyhow she'd guessed.'

'But does she know you're her half-brother?'

'No. I have taken advice . . . and I am keeping my options open.'

'Raisley Conyngham's advice, by the sound of it.'

'Does it matter whose? It suits me very well. I have a plan.'

'Marius. You must not . . . interfere with Tessa.'

'I don't intend to. But she might want to interfere with me. Some years ago, she was quite keen.'

'Not now, never now, not when she has Thea Canteloupe.'

'There could be complications in that area,' said Marius. 'Thea has had a daughter. Suppose Canteloupe wants her to try again for a son? Thea doesn't like men. That puts me off Thea. But with Tessa as a kind of catalyst . . . you see the possibilities?'

'You couldn't be so wicked,' said Fielding.

'Hark who's talking,' said Marius. 'I'd be doing no

51

more, probably a great deal less, than Byron did with his half-sister, Augusta.'

'You know very well that Byron is a bad example. I'm not sure I shouldn't warn Tessa myself.'

'I shan't be very fond of you if you do, Fielding.'

'I suppose not. Well, I shan't spoil your sport. But for Christ's sake be careful. And Marius . . .'

'Yes, Fielding?'

'A lot of us would be quite pleased if you would just settle down and be a normal, decent schoolboy. That way you've got everything going for you, as they say these days. Why not leave all this . . . truffling in the dirt . . . to the pigs?'

'Getting sentimental about me, Fielding?'

'I always have been. Don't forget, your father gave me my first real chance as a writer.'

'Very well. You deserve an answer. I like truffling, Fielding, because I like truffles.'

'But you can't like the dirt.'

'The dirt is a necessary condition of what I have learned to call "the world's game". The most amusing and exciting game of them all, Fielding.'

There was a bleeping on the line.

'Time's run out,' said Marius; and then, as the bleeping paused, 'quite a common occurrence during the world's game. The great question, of course, is when it's going to run out for good. Don't forget to ring up Terpsichore,' he yelled, as the bleeping began again.

Carmilla Salinger wrote from Lancaster College, Cambridge:

'. . . the team is to meet at Piero Caspar's house in the fens. Come by tea time, Friday, prepared to spend a night or two.'

Friday was the next day but one. Fielding could have

left Buttock's Hotel in the charge of Maisie's Assistant Manager, but he neither liked nor trusted the man, so,

'Is that Terpsichore?' he said, when the telephone was answered at the Sterns' London number.

'Who wants her?' said a light masculine voice.

'My name is Fielding Gray . . .'

'*The* Fielding Gray?'

'If such there be. Marius Stern says we should meet.'

'Such a kind boy, Marius. Is he trying to bring us together, do you think?'

'Only with a view to discussing the temporary management of Buttock's Hotel.'

'It would be a change, darling. I've been living here alone for years. Nobody ever comes, except occasionally that cute little Marius. Not so little these days, either. Or quite so cute, come to that.'

'We are talking about Buttock's Hotel.'

'Don't be so stern, darling; it doesn't suit your voice. Makes you sound all mardy. Of course I'm interested in Buttock's – excuse the pun. But I'd have to go on spending some time here. Doing the dusting, you know.'

'Why not?' Fielding said. 'Why not, Terpsichore?'

'Another thing: I'm not Terpsichore any more. Too much of a good thing. I thought Procne might do rather well instead. Procne was a cook too, you see.'

'She killed and cooked her own son,' Fielding said.

'And then became a nightingale, at least in one version, and sang about it all night long.'

'I hope you'll refrain from that. What would the staff and the guests call you?'

'What's wrong with Procne? They'd think it was Polish or something?'

'*Mister* Procne?'

'Oh dear me no, darling. Ms. I'm very advanced these

53

days. I come in drag or not at all . . . and I'm a howling feminist.'

The idea of a transvestite male feminist as manager(ess?) of Buttock's Hotel was more, Fielding thought, than he could resist. If the appointment was a flop, he could take it out on Marius.

'I'm going into the country on Friday,' Fielding said. 'Come and see me at eleven A.M. tomorrow, Thursday.'

'I'll bring some of your books for you to sign, darling. I must say, I take it very kindly of Marius to recommend me, and I take it very kindly of you to follow it up.'

'One thing must be clear, though, Ms Procne. Drag is quite all right with me: but *no dragging back*.'

'No dragging back yourself, *Mister* Gray.'

'Major. Major Gray.'

'So you still use the title?' said Ms Procne. '*Res Unius, Res Omnium*, Major Gray.'

'What?'

'Not forgotten the old motto, have you? And I hope you haven't forgotten me – when you see me. Geddes. Barber of the 10th Sabre Squadron.'*

'Geddes. You cut Daniel Mond's hair before the big manoeuvre, Armageddon – excuse the pun. Geddes. You know that some years after Germany I was blown up in Cyprus? My face is rather a mess. I'm just warning you so as not to give you a nasty shock tomorrow.'

'What happened to your hair? Your lovely auburn hair?'

'Still there, most of it.'

'You'll let me cut it again, as I used to in Göttingen? Just once, for old times' sake.'

'We'll have to see. It doesn't grow as quickly as it did. Seldom needs cutting now.'

* See *The Sabre Squadron* by S. R. (Blond & Briggs, 1966)

A bit of a lie, he thought. Perhaps it would serve. Funny how odd men's memories are, he thought, as he confirmed tomorrow's appointment and rang off. Geddes had remembered his hair – which on no account, however, had he ever been allowed to cut. Officers of the 10th Sabre Squadron did not use the services of the Squadron barber. They went to an elegant Salon in Hanover, taking a whole day off for the purpose.

Why, Fielding wondered, does Carmilla have to choose Piero Caspar's house, in the middle of the distressful fens in the middle of distressful winter, for this conference of hers? Anywhere else in England – in the world – would have been preferable.

On the other hand, he thought, the house, Tunne Hall, had always been a comfortable one even in the knock-about days of the former owner, Ptolemaeos Tunne; and Piero, as his adopted heir, had made many improvements. One no longer ate in the kitchen; the heating had been improved until it was a match for the fenland dews and fogs; the two appalling witches that had cooked and kept were gone for ever; and the place was now manned by a deaf and dumb Jack of all work (crude but serviceable) and by a trio of courteous if sometimes rather voluble male cot-queans from Syracuse. If, thought Fielding, Maisie should return to Buttock's and have no use for Ms Procne (duly installed as Manageress the previous day), I shall seriously recommend to Piero that he takes Procne on to control his crew of Sicels. Apart from anything else, Procne's cooking, of which he had been given a special example last night in Buttock's, by far excelled the South Italian cuisine provided by the present cook, Luigino, sound as this doubtless was. Luigino could no more attempt Procne's eggs in lobster sauce under a covering of cheese soufflé than he could swim back to Sicily (not that he'd want to, for although all the Sicilians found the fens abominable, they adored Piero and were paid munificently). It would be interesting to see whether Maisie would be minded to keep Ms Procne on at Buttock's after she returned . . . *if* she returned, thought Fielding miserably, remembering the dismal report he had received on the telephone a few hours earlier from La Soeur's successor in the nursing home where Maisie lay, silent and motionless once more, as she had been when her illness started.

But suddenly the sun shone on the fields as Fielding drove, and the light, bright frost was merry about him, so he put away his sorrowful thoughts of his long-time friend, kind Maisie, and thought of the welcome with which Caspar would meet him at Tunne Hall. Who else would be there? Carmilla, the convener, of course, and probably Jeremy. That would make, with Piero Caspar, four acknowledged experts on Marius. Didn't they need, then, an acknowledged expert on Raisley Conyngham, the enemy? But of acknowledged experts (as opposed to casual gossip-mongers) about Raisley Conyngham there were very few, and these did not turn up at conferences to discuss the undoing of Raisley.

Jeremy Morrison drove from Luffham-by-Whereham through Swaffham and Downham Market to Upmill Fen and Christchurch, through Manea (not as pleasant a place as it sounded), Welches Dam and Chatteris, where he took the B1050 across Pidley Fen to Pidley. Soon after this he turned right and proceeded a little way towards the Isle of Ely (where the monks of the Palatinate, he remembered, had greeted King Cnut with a hearty anthem), and then south a little way to Witchford, and so on to Tunne Hall, where two of the cot-queans from Syracuse marched out of the front door, together and abreast, to attend ceremoniously to his luggage; for although there was very little of this, his style of 'Honourable' elevated him, in their view, to the status of 'milor Inglese', and no service could be too assiduous for such a wondrous being.

Carmilla drove over to Tunne Hall from Cambridge, fairly early in the afternoon as she did not (these days) like motoring alone in the dark. This was not because she couldn't see well enough to drive, but because when the dark came down some old faces came out of it (her adopted mother's or Baby Canteloupe's) which she did not wish to see.

I might have asked Fielding to pick me up in Cambridge on his way from London, she thought, or even made Jeremy take a long deviation from Luffham. But then I should not have had my own car with me, and, since I do not wish to be dependent either on Fielding, Jeremy or Piero, that would have been a nuisance and a bore.

'So,' said Carmilla by the fire in the library: 'tell us, Piero, what you think of Marius' behaviour while he was with you in Italy.'

'Good company. Prepared to defend his treacherous mission, but still not entirely certain, I think, that he would go through with it – fair-minded enough to listen patiently, from time to time, to the arguments I urged against it.'

'What hope did you have that he might drop his original purpose?'

'Very little, but not none at all. In the event, as we all know, he simply came too late to Brindisi to pursue the matter.'

'Jeremy,' Carmilla said: 'did you see Marius at all in Brindisi?'

'He paid a courtesy visit to the hospital where I was,' said Jeremy. 'Fielding was there, and Piero. Not an occasion for searching discussion. But we spoke very closely, Marius and I, while we were in the Peloponnese together after Christmas. The sum of it all is that Marius claims to have his own genius or *daimon* which makes him morally independent. He has listened to Raisley's lessons, he says, both about literature and about life, and has been much informed and impressed by them; but in the end it is his *daimon*, not Raisley, that tells him what to do. One felt bound to comment that the *daimon*'s instructions seemed to bear a remarkable resemblance to what we know, or have good cause to suspect, might so easily be Raisley Conyngham's. Marius' *daimon* appears to have a lot of Raisley's style.'

'And did Marius agree,' asked Carmilla, 'that his *daimon* had been influenced or even formed by Raisley?'

'No. He said that it was, perhaps, his own part of God.'

'If he said that and meant it,' said Piero, 'he can surely be left on his own to fight his own battle.'

'No,' said Fielding Gray. 'I have spoken to him, on the telephone, since he has been home from Greece . . . since he has gone back to school where he is taught by Raisley Conyngham. His attitudes have already deteriorated from those described by Jeremy and Piero. For example. He had received certain confidences from Mrs Malcolm when she was on the verge of a mental breakdown. He is now considering the possibility of exploiting these for his own pleasure or advantage.'

Fielding now told the company what Marius had learned from Maisie and what he was apparently prepared to make of it.

'He had telephoned me,' Fielding said, 'to make sure that Maisie was speaking the truth – that Tessa was indeed her child and fathered by Gregory Stern, and was therefore Marius' half-sister. Now, Tessa herself has somehow surmised, it seems, that Maisie is her mother; but she does *not* know that Marius is her half-brother. Nor does Marius now propose to tell her. He is, in his own phrase, keeping his options open . . . in case he wishes to exploit her in a fashion which she might not allow if she knew their true relation. In order not to annoy him, I have reluctantly condoned his attitude. We have to co-operate with him . . . up to a point . . . if we are to get anywhere with him.'

'Not up to the point of allowing him to exploit, as you call it, his own sister,' Carmilla said.

'It is not quite what you imagine. Marius thinks that if Canteloupe wants your sister, Theodosia, to conceive again in hope of a boy, then Tessa can help to bring about this conception, by acting as a kind of catalyst (Marius' phrase again) between Marius and Thea. You see, their feelings are now such, Marius' and Thea's, that they would not come together with a good will, or indeed at all, unless some such . . . enticement . . . was to operate on them.'

'For a start,' said Carmilla coolly, 'Teresa must be warned that Marius is her brother.'

'Half-brother,' Piero said. 'It makes a difference, as we used to say in Syracuse.'

'Teresa must be warned,' repeated Carmilla.

'Marius has told me,' said Fielding, 'that if Tessa is told that he is her half-brother, he will be very displeased.'

'Then he must be displeased,' said Carmilla.

'We shall get nowhere without his trust. It would be better if you, Carmilla, tell your sister, Theodosia, and leave her to make sure that nothing untoward should occur. She is a capable woman, Thea, and can easily manage this. What is perhaps more to the point,' said

Fielding, 'is that Marius' perverse attitude in all this is almost certainly based on Conyngham's advice. I put this to Marius, and he did not try to deny it.'

'What has been happening,' said Jeremy, 'to this *daimon* which Marius is so pleased with?'

'I think that its light has diminished since he rejoined his master, Raisley, at school.'

'What you are saying,' said Carmilla, 'is that whether or not Marius' *daimon* is a part of God, Raisley Conyngham is certainly part of the Devil, and that Marius, *daimon* or no *daimon*, is too weak to resist him. As we have so often said in the past, Conyngham must be driven out. Yet, as we have also said, he is a respectable schoolmaster of long service, and his teaching of the classics has produced unimpeachable results. So how is he to be driven out? It must be evident now that this is what we have to decide. First,' she said, rising and walking over to a shelf of reference books, 'one must know one's enemy.'

She took down a recent edition of *Who's Who*.

'Let us now consider the official *curriculum vitae* of Raisley Conyngham.'

'It is surely the unofficial parts with which we are most concerned,' Piero Caspar said.

'Precisely,' said Carmilla; 'but we shall best begin to find those by looking through the gaps in the rest. Now then' – she flipped the pages – '"CONYNGHAM, Raisley Moffat Windsor: b. 1936,"' she read, '"s. of late Tewkesbury Moffat Conyngham, of Ullacote in the county of Somerset, esquire."

'Rather an elaborate way of referring to one's dead father,' commented Carmilla; 'and I see he lists no mother. Rather odd.'

'Lots of people don't,' said Fielding, 'I didn't myself. It

generally means that they didn't like her (as in my case) or that their father had married beneath him.'

'"Educ.: Brydales, and Marcian College, Cambridge (BA [Hons. Cantab.] 1956; MA [Cantab.] 1960). Second Lieutenant, The Blue Mowbrays, 1956–8." Hmmm,' said Carmilla; 'National Service, of course.'

'He must have been one of the very last to do it,' said Fielding: 'I must say, he seems to have got his commission very quickly – probably sent straight to OCTU because he was a graduate.'

'After his Service he went to teach at your school,' said Carmilla. 'Started in 1959. He is described here as having become, in 1972, "Mag. Sec. Lit. Hum." and in 1976 "Baro vers. Lat. et Graec." What on earth does all that mean?'

'Second Master of Classics,' said Jeremy, 'and Baron of Latin and Greek Verse.'

'Baron? What an extraordinary title, in the context.'

'Not really. Like calling somebody Lord of Misrule or King of the Toasts and Cups. Barons of the Verse or Verses,' said Fielding. 'What's wrong with that? Rather splendid.'

'I find it most touching and appropriate,' said Piero, 'this loyalty to your old school. Try this port: I have just bought a dozen cases from Berry Bros and should value your advice.'

'Nothing very sinister or out of the way so far,' said Carmilla, rapping the pages of *Who's Who* '. . . though rather fancy about his dead father's having been squire of Ullacote, and very finicking about his degree at Cambridge.'

'Schoolmasters have to be finicking about their degrees,' said Fielding. 'Paying parents expect it. What's this place, Brydales, he went to before 'Varsity?'

'A co-educational crank school in the West Country,'

said Jeremy. 'My brother Nickie was sent there as a forlorn hope when his brain started to soften. I can't think Raisley was taught much Latin and Greek there.'

'There used to be a famous female at Brydales,' said Carmilla, 'who taught Latin and Greek very vividly – to anyone who wished to learn. So if he'd been well grounded at his prep. school and liked the classics, he'd have had an ideal instructor. Perhaps, if he was a delicate boy (more than likely), his father taught him before he went to Brydales. A man called Tewkesbury Conyngham – it must be the same one – was famous in the thirties as a classical archaeologist and roving antiquary. The war would have brought him home in good time to teach little Raisley, and it sounds from his previous career as if he might have been rather an exciting teacher.

'But we shall be going into all such details later,' said Carmilla: 'myself, I very much look forward to finding out a lot more about Miss Jesty Hyphen, the Classical Mistress at Brydales. There is a big question mark over her name: she had to retire early, but the secret behind that was so well kept that no one ever found out why. Meanwhile . . . let us note that *Who's Who* makes no mention of Raisley's string of horses – bad publicity for a schoolmaster, I suppose – but does mention a sabbatical year in the mid-seventies, just before he became "Baron of Latin and Greek Verse". Apparently he was offered a grant by his old College, Marcian, to do what is described as "Ecclesiastical Research in the Languedoc", and your school gave him a year off to go and do it. Generous – though I expect it was without pay. And so what, we ask ourselves, was Raisley sniffing after in the Languedoc in 1975? The whole thing was obviously pretty prestigious, since his old college sponsored him and the school at which he taught was prepared to release him. And yet, unless I am very much mistaken, nothing has been heard about this research since.'

'A gap,' said Fielding, 'of the kind we are looking for. The entry records the expedition – of which nothing further is known. Why is the entry there then? It would not be like Raisley to record a flop. There must be more to this than appears here.'

'I hope that this and other matters will soon be made very plain,' said Carmilla, 'when we look closer. Now then. Division of tasks. Fielding, the old soldier, to find out what he can about Raisley's time as a National Serviceman in the Blue Mowbrays – and the period during which he was being trained for his commission. Fielding and Jeremy to pursue Raisley's career at Marcian College, Cambridge. Myself to assist them with local knowledge. Piero and I to look at his time at Brydales (with special reference to Jesty Hyphen, who must have taught him), at his early years at Ullacote, and at the character and achievements of his father, from whom Raisley may (or may not) have received his early education. Myself and Piero also to investigate what condition Ullacote is in at the present time, along with Raisley's string of National Hunt horses; and Jeremy and Fielding to make enquiries about Raisley's performances as a Classics Master at their old school and the general impression which he has made over the years. *Particular notice* to be taken both at the school and at Marcian College of anything that may still be known of Raisley's sabbatical year and the "Ecclesiastical Research" which he attempted.

'Finally,' said Carmilla, 'if my instinct is right, we shall all of us, having learned whatever we may and pooled our knowledge, have to set out together to the Languedoc to follow up the expedition which Raisley undertook. There can be, in my view, no proper plan made by us until full acount has been taken of the sabbatical year and whatever

63

Raisley was engaged in, "Ecclesiastical Research" or something other, during the course of it. The item about this sabbatical year is for our purposes the most suggestive in his entire entry. It must surely be probable that anything . . . anything which he might wish to hide . . . occurred during the year he spent in the Languedoc, during the period of the so called "research", the date and auspices of which have been so prominently recorded but of the *substance* of which not one jot or tittle has apparently been published since.'

'Tomorrow,' said Piero, 'will be time enough for us to consider the details of our journeys and enquiries. Meanwhile,' he said, filling liberal glasses of the Taylor '49 from Berry Bros, 'what shall we drink to to mark our assembly here?'

'To the final downfall and departure of Raisley Conyngham?' said Fielding Gray.

'To the final salvation of Marius Stern?' said Jeremy Morrison.

'To the discovery of the truth?' said Piero Caspar.

'To none of these,' said Carmilla Salinger as she raised her glass: 'but to the art and pleasure of the Hunt.'

'To the art and pleasure of the Hunt,' they cried; then drained their glasses in one and, led by Piero (to whom, after all, the very expensive glasses belonged), flung them into the grate.

PART TWO
Cathar Country

It sited was in fruitful soyle of old,
And girt in with two walls on either side;
The one of yron, the other of bright gold.
That none might thorough break, nor overstride:
And double gates it had which opened wide,
By which both in and out men moten pas:
Th' one faire and fresh, the other old and dride.
Old Genius the porter of them was,
Old Genius, the which a double nature has . . .

(Edmund Spenser, *The Faerie Queen*,
Book III, Canto VI, Stanza xxxi)

. . . And all about grew every sort of flowre,
To which sad lovers were transformde of yore;
Fresh Hyacinthus, Phoebus paramoure
And dearest love;
Foolish Narcisse, that likes the watry shore;
Sad Amaranthus, made a flowre but late,
Sad Amaranthus, in whose purple gore
Me seems I see Amintas wretched fate,
To whom sweete Poets verse hath given endlesse date.

There wont fair Venus often to enjoy
Her deare Adonis joyous company,
And reape sweet pleasure of the wanton boy:
There yet, some say, in secret he does ly,
Lapped in flowres and pretious spycery,
By her hid from the world, and from the skill
Of Stygian Gods, which do her love envy;
Put she her selfe, when ever that she will,
Possesseth him, and of his sweetnesse takes her fill.

Ibidem, Stanzas xlv and xlvi

Since Tunne Hall was so close to Cambridge, they started their search with enquiries about Raisley Conyngham's time at Marcian College.

'An ancient and obscure college,' Carmilla said to Jeremy and Fielding, 'with two Eton Fives courts. Marcian was a rather successful Emperor of the Roman Empire of the East round the middle of the fifth century A.D. There is no conceivable reason why a college should have been named after him, except that he had the misfortune to preside over Byzantium when it was split from top to bot by the monophysite controversy – which had to do with the relationship between the Father and the Son. Were they of the same substance or of a similar substance?'

'The old Arian squabble?'

'With knobs on,' said Carmilla. 'Was Christ both human and divine? Could he get an erection? That kind of a thing.'

'To which party did the Emperor Marcian incline?'

'To the party of common sense. He was principally interested in promoting peace and quiet, which, in practice, meant dowsing extremists, with which Constantinople was absolutely heaving, of all persuasions.'

'He sounds rather a good chap,' said Jeremy.

'By a perverse association,' said Carmilla, 'the college named after him has always particularly favoured theologians – though this was the very class that had turned his reign into a nightmare. The college has a famous library of theology and divinity known as the Chalcedonian

Library, in memory of the Oecumenical Council of Chalcedon, which made a series of moderate pronouncements in religious affairs.'

'How extraordinary,' said Jeremy. 'I hardly knew Marcian existed when I was up. Where is it?'

'Near the Round Church.'

'Where one used to get taxis? I never noticed a college round there.'

'That is hardly surprising,' said Carmilla. 'The entrance gate is very humble, and is half-way down one of those squalid alleyways behind the church – the one that leads to the pawnbroker's near Portugal Place. So there you are, boys: you are now supplied with information historical, academical and topographical: off you go.'

'Which is all very well,' said Fielding to Jeremy; 'but where does one start?'

Fielding had never attended a university: Jeremy had.

'One starts with the head porter,' Jeremy said. 'After all, Conyngham was there only twenty-five years ago. Head porters go on for ever.'

The head porter of Marcian was a brisk forty-five years old, having started his career at the age of twenty and been promoted over the heads of his seniors (though of course Fielding and Jeremy were not to know this) because he cherished a nasty little secret about the Master's second daughter, who had been allowed access to certain crucial papers, on certain crural conditions, just before Part II of her Tripos. Mr Trapp ('Call me plain "Trapp", gentlemen: "Mister", these days, is merely common') was of military cut and civil speech. Yes, he remembered Raisley Conyngham; yes, he would show the gentlemen Conyngham's old rooms. He had been junior porter but one when Conyngham was up and had frequently carried parcels there. Conyngham was rich and had a lot of interesting parcels. He, Trapp, had therefore remembered the man (weedy but well groomed, with an Edwardian air) and remembered his rooms (expensively furnished – Conyngham was probably the last gentleman in the college to have furnished his rooms himself). And here they were; now occupied by one of the Junior Fellows, who was away on some footling conference. Not as spick as they had been in Conyngham's time; downright sloppy in fact; not even clean; he must have a word with the stair slut (Marcian usage for bedmaker) about that. But you could tell the status which Conyngham had enjoyed as an undergraduate from the fact that he'd had rooms that were now thought good enough for a Fellow – albeit a Junior Fellow and a scruffy little Geordie at that. What gave Conyngham that status? Money and intelligence. He was not much liked. He had, however, one close friend, a certain Prideau Glastonbury, with whom he shared an interest in race horses. They used to go to Newmarket together, which was in those days forbidden, if only as a matter of form.

'Your memory of the early fifties seems admirably clear, Trapp,' said Fielding Gray.

'Raisley Conyngham was about the only thing remotely memorable, sir,' said Trapp. 'This, as you may know, is the least distinguished college in the kingdom, with the possible exception of Hertford College, Oxford – which did at least produce an author called Evelyn Waugh.'

'Well then,' said Jeremy, 'if your memories of Conyngham are so vivid, perhaps you will recall that nearly twenty years after he went down this college sponsored him to undertake "research" in the South of France.'

'No, sir. "Research" is not my business.'

'Then whose business?'

'The registrar may be able to help you. If Raisley Conyngham is a rich man, gentlemen – and I notice from

69

the sporting press that his horses run from time to time on the turf – why could he not have sponsored his own "research"?'

'A very good question, Trapp. Thank you for the tour,' said Jeremy, who now produced a five pound note in his left hand and a ten pound note in his right, and examined them both alternately, in a solemn and scholarly manner. 'Tell me, Trapp: did Conyngham ever invite ladies to his room?'

'No, sir, not even in May week. He never attended a College Ball. Yet he was a handsome young man in a slightly sallow way. All the stair sluts fancied him rotten. They thought he was "interesting", you see. But from the look of him as he walked through the college and into the street he fancied nobody nor nothing. No woman; not the other thing neither.'

Jeremy gave Trapp the tenner. As they went on their way to the registrar, he observed, 'Trapp might easily have tried to make something up to amuse us. Or he might even have been awkward about talking at all. On balance he deserves ten.'

'He's not been a lot of help,' said Fielding, who never liked to see money being given away to other people.

'Swingeing Court, he told us,' said Jeremy, ignoring Fielding's avaricious grouch; 'the registrar is to be found, he said, not in the office area but in Room T 5, Swingeing Court.'

They came into a court no bigger than an Eton Fives court – which, indeed, it had evidently been before the buttress and the ledges had been hopelessly eroded by the gargoyles which spewed from the gutter above.

'Carmilla said two Fives courts,' said Fielding. 'They've certainly let this one go to rack. T 5 in that corner. No mention of the registrar.'

They ascended one flight of stairs and knocked. A small

whiny voice bade them enter. Inside they found a creature like the shrivelled Sibyl of Cumae (who had to be kept in a birdcage, Fielding remembered, for her own protection). The registrar (if he it was) sat on a hard chair, his feet barely reaching the floor, and looked plaintively into a wheezing gas fire.

'What do you want?' whined the Sibyl who appeared, by courtesy of dress, to be of the male sex.

'You are the registrar, sir?' said Jeremy.

'So I believe. Doctor Davie Gamp, DD.' He held up a small notebook. 'What would you wish me to register? The files and so on are in my office. I go there at dead of night to transfer information from this book. My office overlooks the street, you see, and the noise disturbs me. That is why the Fives court outside is not used any more. Even the patter of a Fives ball would drive me mad.'

'Couldn't you have found another room?' said Fielding, failing to see why the legitimate pastimes of the under-graduates should be abandoned for the convenience of this unattractive personage.

'This is the smallest and most remote of Marcian's Courts, and therefore the least raucous . . . provided, of course, that there are no Sphaeric games like Fives, which are in any case prohibited by a college statute of 1515.'

'Notwithstanding which,' said Fielding, 'I hope they still play in the other college Fives court.'

'I believe they are erecting a women's latrine on it. We are to have females, you see. None of which concerns you, unless you are connected with the college. What would you wish to register? Perhaps you wish to put down the names of your sons? I'm afraid the college does not reserve places on that basis any more. Even if you are old members of the college – which you are not, or I should know you – I could not keep places for your sons. There is now some kind of examination which determines the matter.'

'Surely,' said Jeremy, 'there always was.'

'Oh yes. But if someone we liked the look of failed it, we took no notice. Now this is no longer possible. Unlike the Provost of Lancaster, the Master of Marcian is not sovereign within his college. Officials and politicians – even welfare workers – can interfere with him.'

'I was at Lancaster,' said Jeremy. 'The interference there was of another kind.'

'Indeed?'

'The late Provost, Sir Tom Llewyllyn,' said Jeremy, thinking the Sibyl would enjoy this and co-operate in consequence, 'believed that the tree nymphs from the felled trees of the College Avenue still lingered to haunt and curse the place.'

'Tom Llewyllyn was a fool.'

'We stand here for him,' Fielding said.

'I know from reading his books. Exercises in one form or another of velleity – Socialist velleity when he was young and hot. Laodicean velleity when he was comfortable and middle-aged. Or take the absurdity of his marriage. He married the elder of the Turbot girls, Patricia. A nephew of mine was at the wedding. Jonathan Gamp; nasty catamite. He should have known – Llewyllyn, I mean, not my nephew Jonathan – that the Turbots were bad stock. Matter for Bedlam. The younger girl, Isobel, set fire to the house and eloped on her sister's wedding day.* What sort of behaviour do you call that? And I gather they put Patricia away years ago, because she chewed a boy's ear off.† So what sort of behaviour do you call *that*?'

---

* See *Friends in Low Places* by S. R. (Anthony Blond, 1965)
† See *The Survivors* by S. R. (Blond & Briggs, 1976)

After a brief silence, Doctor Gamp waved his notebook in the air.

'What information would you wish me to record?' he asked.

'On the contrary, sir. We would wish you to give some information to us. Does the name Raisley Conyngham mean anything to you?'

'Oh yes.'

'Then what do you know of this man's being sponsored, by this college, in the mid-seventies, to undertake a year's research in southern France . . . in the Languedoc?'

'Fudge,' said Doctor Gamp, DD: 'fudge, fudge, fudge.'

'You mean,' said Fielding, 'that the thing was spurious in some way?'

'Conyngham wanted a year away from that school at which he was teaching without prejudice to his future career there. It was therefore important to him that the sabbatical leave which he was about to request should appear to be for the most prestigious purpose. It occurred to him that the school might believe this if we at Marcian said we were prepared to sponsor his research.'

'You mean, prepared to fund his research?' Jeremy said.

'Prepared in some fashion to support it. We could say that we were sponsoring his research if, for example, we gave him a set of rooms for a few weeks and the free run of our libraries. Since Raisley Conyngham's research apparently had to do with theological controversy and religious deviation, our Chalcedonian Library, which specializes in such matters, would be an appropriate place of preparation for his task.'

'Why bother with the man at all?'

'We bothered, because Conyngham's proposition to us was as follows: he was planning, he said, a serious project of research into medieval heresies; would we, in return

73

for a very handsome donation towards the upkeep of the Chalcedonian Library, permit him to live in college, with dining rights, and work in the Chalcedonian Library all through the Long Vacation of 1975? Yes, said the College Council: we would.

'So you see,' whined Davie Gamp, 'Conyngham was able to tell the Governing Body of his school that the Council of his old College was so impressed by his plans for research that it was prepared to give him the privileges of a Fellow for four whole months, from early June to the beginning of October, in order that he might live in the peaceful precinct of the college, within convenient distance of the college's famous theological library, which would be thrown open to him. He then, he said to the Governors of the school, wished to spend eight months researching in "the field" in Provence and the Languedoc, which would bring him to the end of May 1976. After this he would devote himself to two things – to the collation of his findings in the south of France, and to preparation for his duties in the appointment of "Baro vers. Lat. et Graec." – "Baron of Latin and Greek Verses" – which, as was already known, he was to take up in the autumn of 1976. All this I learned from the Honorary Senior Usher of the School, with whom I had been for many years in correspondence. He was no longer a working member of the school staff, but he was still very much of the place and occasionally gave lectures on Art and Literature.'

'Now dead, alas,' said Fielding. 'A pity. I should have enjoyed discussing all this with him.'

'Not a lot to discuss, in the end,' said Gamp, who sounded like a moribund cicada. 'The school consented to release Raisley Conyngham for four Quarters, Cricket Quarter '75 to Cricket Quarter '76, inclusive, without pay. After that Conyngham would take up his appointment as "Baro". The Governors felt rather flattered that a master in their classical department should be doing research under the aegis of Marcian College – little knowing that Conyngham was indirectly paying for the college's support by a substantial anonymous gift to the funds of the Chalcedonian. As for the actual *results* of the research, it was appreciated that it is always a very long time before such work is published, and the Governors were happy as long as they deemed the Council of Marcian to be happy. The Council of Marcian, for their part, were entirely satisfied with Conyngham's seigneurial gift, honoured their agreement about accommodation and the rest, and gave never the faintest goddamn about the outcome of the research, which had never in practice concerned them.'

'They did, however,' said Jeremy, 'appear to the public to be sponsoring it?'

'To what public? Only to the Governors of that school and to a tiny group of academics, who could find nothing extraordinary if publication of the research were deferred for a generation or for ever. True, my correspondent, the Honorary Senior Usher, smelt something a bit whiffy, but he had long been supernumerary and now, as one of you has just observed, is dead.'

'But surely,' said Fielding, 'there must have been some research. Raisley Conyngham must have wanted all that time off, including four months here in Marcian, for *something*. Otherwise he would hardly have paid out all that money to provide a convincing scenario. He did come here that Long Vac? And read in the Chalcedonian?'

'Certainly he did. I found his company at High Table most sustaining. Not many dons stay here during the Long Vacation, as you may know, and those that do are for the most part specialized scientists of narrow discourse. Raisley Conyngham commanded any kind of table talk one had a mind to.'

'Did he speak of his research?'

'He was only preparing for it at this stage, you should remember. But he spoke of its purposed scope and nature: late developments of the Cathar or Albigensian Heresy – that most fascinating of Dualisms – with particular reference to the Demiurge, who made the material universe, or, as some would call him, the Devil.'

'And how did he get on,' said Jeremy, 'when he arrived in "the field" in Provence and the Languedoc?'

'I never heard,' said Doctor Gamp. 'No more did anyone else. When I said goodbye to him at the beginning of October, 1975, I urged him to keep me posted – so intrigued had I become by some of his speculations. But never, from that day to this, had I any word more from him.'

'Well then: can you remember any of his speculations?'

'Oh yes,' chirruped Gamp morosely; 'but I'm not going to tell them to you two. You mean Raisley harm, don't you? I can see it in your mean, prying faces. You want to raise discredit or scandal against him – I should have realized earlier. But I see little company these days and am prone to chatter when I have an audience; and now my tongue has flown out of my head.'

'No harm done. You have only confirmed what we already surmised – that Raisley's Conyngham's "research" wasn't quite as respectable as it seemed to be from the reference to it in *Who's Who*; that it might have been a cover for something else . . . when he got into "the field".'

'Ah. That's more than we know, isn't it? None of us was there in "the field" with him. He has published no results, as far as we apprehend, reputable or disreputable, true or false. Nothing to go on for any of us. We don't even know where, in the Languedoc, he went – or whether he went there at all. He went away in October, 1975, and came back to England in May of 1976. That's all anybody knows. Tee-hee,' said Doctor Gamp, DD. 'You clever young man, and you clever middle-aged one – you know not a tittle more than silly old senile Gamp.'

'And of course,' said Carmilla Salinger to Fielding and Jeremy in Piero Caspar's rooms that evening, 'he's quite right.'

Piero Caspar was a Fellow of Lancaster as well as Squire of Tunne Hall. He had caused the college kitchens to produce a very passable dinner for four, which had started with caviar (beluga at that) and was now ending with bone marrow on fried bread.

'So,' Piero said now: 'before we start investigating Conyngham's research we first need to confirm that he ever did it?'

'We know,' said Fielding, 'that he studied in the Chalcedonian for four months, and that he studied the Albigensians.'

'We *think* he studied the Albigensians,' said Carmilla. 'The fact that he told poor old Gamp that he was doing so means nothing. He might have been reading anything in that library. Before we can proceed we must know exactly what he was up to and exactly where he really intended to go. We should have a very good chance of finding further clues at Ullacote – servants' gossip and so on – and at the school on Farncombe Hill. After all, he must have communicated with somebody there about his progress. We must find out what reports he sent in. If they were true, good. If they were false then so much the better, because once established to be so they should lead to significant inference.'

'The Manor of Ullacote,' mused Jeremy, 'and the old school on Farncombe Hill . . . So you think that we need no longer bother with Raisley's time at Brydales or in the Army?'

'I think nothing of the kind. I said Ullacote and the school were the most likely places to yield clues, not the only ones.'

'It is difficult to see,' said Jeremy, 'how anyone now at Brydales, even if Raisley is still remembered there after thirty years, can tell us much about his activities in 1975 and 1976. Much the same must apply to the Blue Mowbrays – a regiment that is in any case extinct.'

'I still think that Miss Jesty Hyphen, formerly senior Classical Mistress at Brydales, might have some pertinent things to tell us,' Carmilla said.

'Giles Glastonbury,' said Fielding.

'What about him?'

'A regular soldier.'

'But not, surely, in the Blue Mowbrays?'

'No. But he may well have had a hand in getting Raisley Conyngham a commission in that regiment. Raisley Conyngham knew Prideau Glastonbury, Giles's cousin, when they were both up at Cambridge. I remember Giles's telling me, some time back, that Raisley was introduced to him by Prideau, as a fellow enthusiast for racing and, in general, as someone of a kind that Giles might find "useful" as the years went on. And in fact Raisley has since done Giles several good turns (Giles told me), one of them being to accept an old friend of Giles as his private trainer; but the point is that these good turns were done in recognition of what Giles had previously done for Raisley, in order to put Raisley under obligation and keep his name on Giles's books as a potentially "useful" fellow. The great thing that Giles did for Raisley was to stop his being axed from OCTU when he was an officer cadet in 1956. Raisley had disgraced himself by being feeble on an important exercise on Dartmoor, and was quite rightly about to lose his cadetship; but Giles, then in the War Office, managed to interfere on Raisley's behalf and bring him safely off with a commission. It is therefore not unlikely that it was through Giles's good offices that Raisley (clearly a very doubtful commodity in military terms) was accepted by the Blue Mowbrays. In which case a conversation with Giles Glastonbury might be in order.'

'Very well,' said Carmilla. 'Piero and I will seek out Miss Jesty Hyphen. I have already established from her old college, Newnham, that she is in an old people's home on the coast of Kent. Meanwhile, you and Jeremy, Fielding, had better beard Giles Glastonbury.'

Len, Private Secretary to the Provost of Lancaster, said to Sir Jacquiz Helmutt, the Provost:

'Carmilla Salinger is rounding up a posse to ride after Raisley Conyngham.'

'How do you know?' The Provost looked fiercely through the window of his office and down on to the rear lawn of Lancaster, in the middle of which three female undergraduates were lasciviously kissing, contrary to any number of regulations. 'Who told you this about Miss Salinger?'

'Miss Salinger did. She wanted a little advice.'

'And you gave it?' said Sir Jacquiz, watching with interest as the senior college gardener approached the erotic group in the centre of the lawn.

'I told her to leave Conyngham alone. He was no threat to her, I told her. She said he was a threat to Marius Stern. I reminded her that Marius was quite tough enough to take care of himself. But she has a heavy maternal crush on the boy, so that was no good.'

'Do we much mind if Carmilla rides the range in pursuit of Conyngham?'

The senior gardener doffed his cap to the three osculants. It now became apparent that one of these was not a female but a long-haired androgyne.

'We don't much mind, Provost. But she's got interesting academic work in hand, and I wish she'd get on with her book. If she doesn't produce something soon, one of your lovely left-wing council will try to do her the dirt and fuck up her Fellowship. They hate her, you see, for being rich.'

The two females and the androgyne languished round the gardener. The scene began to look like a Burne-Jones. The gardener, however, now spurned his worshippers and drove them away before him with a small three-pronged fork, which he had produced from his left-leg gumboot. More trouble to come from the Student Union, thought Provost Helmutt: a motion condemning the fascist attitudes of the college servants. But it had been worth it. The three faces of the undergraduates who were being driven towards the window in which he sat were memorably contorted, like those of a crowd in panic rendered by Munch.

'If anyone makes trouble for Carmilla,' said the Provost, 'we can always accuse him of being anti-feminist or sexist or something of the sort.'

'Clever Provost. But suppose it's one of the female Fellows that turns nasty?'

'Then we say she's lacking in female solidarity and in proper loyalty to her own minority group.'

'Clever Provost,' cooed Len once more. 'Len likes it. Len likes it a lot. All the same, Carmilla should steer clear of Raisley Conyngham and get on with her work. As I say, he's no threat to her just now, but if she starts provoking him, well, Conyngham can be most disagreeable, Provost, quite diabolically disagreeable.'

'How disagreeable is that?'

'You have read the novel of Balzac in which somebody dies because the arch-crook has touched his head and sent poison down the tubes of his hair and into his blood stream?'

'Yes. Sheer rubbish.'

'So you may say, learned Provost, but that's how nasty Conyngham can get (or so they say) if he's crossed.'

'You are speaking metaphorically?'

'Yes, I hope; but quite possibly no. I have positively heard it alleged, Provost, that Raisley Conyngham has . . . caused at least one person to die in that kind of way. In any case at all, Knightly Provost, he can be a whole lot beastlier than even your beastly left-wing council.'

'Raisley Conyngham,' whinnied Miss Jesty Hyphen: 'best boy I ever taught at Brydales. Not that that was saying much, because the standard was appalling, and the children were all the pampered brats of silly rich socialists . . . the sort of children that said, "I wanna be an artist", or, "I wanna be an orchestral conductor", and expected to be transformed into Augustus John or Constant Lambert in a matter of minutes.'

Miss Jesty Hyphen was a tiny little woman wrapped in a tartan rug and rolled into a ball and set on an invalid chair out of which, one felt, she might inadvertently bounce at any moment. With Carmilla and Piero on either side of her, she was parked on the veranda, full in the fierce sea breeze, of Aesculapius House, a discreet home for old women on the Promenade at Hythe. ('Welcome to Aesculapius House,' she had greeted Carmilla and Piero when they arrived: 'it's not here for health but for death; yet not such a bad place to die in.') And now, sitting on the open veranda ('So much the better if I get pneumonia and cease being a bloody nuisance in the world'), she was talking of Brydales and Raisley Conyngham's adolescence there.

'A thin, pretty, delicate little thing,' said Miss Jesty. 'Voice didn't break till very late, I remember. I once saw his pego; tiny little thing like a snail, very neatly circumcised, not a hair in sight, though he was already over fifteen. And just in case you think I ramped round peering at little boys' pegoes, I should explain that this was when we went on a holiday together one summer and were compelled, much against our wills, to share a bedroom for a couple of nights.'

'A holiday together?' said Carmilla.

'In 1951. As I say, he was the only child in the place who showed any taste for the classics at all. The rest thought they were so superior and talented (for had not their parents and most of the staff perpetually told them they were?) that they wouldn't trouble to learn any grammar. Or anything else for that matter. They just went through the days saying, "I wanna do this", or, "I wanna do that", and always "wanning" to change to something else at the first sign of minor difficulty. But Raisley stuck his nose in his book and kept it there. He turned off splendid copies of prose and verse, and, far better, actually understood the substance of what he was reading. At fourteen and a half he was saying, "But look here, Hyphen" – that's what the children called me – "look here, Hyphen," he was saying in his squeaky voice, "if we wish to appreciate ancient poetry, there's no room at all for the Christian God."'

' "Amen," I said: "you've got it in one. No place for the Christian God and no place for the Christian morality. Christianity and Christian doctrine are cod's wallop," I said – though Brydales was officially a Christian school – "unproven, unprovable, absurd, joyless and obscene . . . a word which comes, mark you, from the Latin '*ob*' and the Latin '*scaenus*', '*obscaenus*', i.e. cluttering up the stage, in the way, a bloody pain." He took the point and throve from then on.'

'Throve so much,' said Piero, 'that you took him on a holiday?'

'His father paid. He wanted Raisley out of the way that summer because he was planning a very special house party at Ullacote, the family seat. Raisley's mother was already dead – no one knew who she was or who she had been, and certainly nobody cared (not even Raisley, who for a time regarded me as his mother), and Raisley's father was giving this house party, and there was no place in it for Raisley.

'"I expect they'll be having orgies," said little Raisley as we drove from Bordeaux towards Pau; "I once watched them at it when they thought I was safe in bed. You never saw anything less attractive, Hyphen."

'"I don't suppose so," I said.

'"Blowsy women with sagging bottoms, stringy men with toe-nails like talons and hairs all over their backs. I love my father, he was a marvellous teacher before you came into my life, but I really do wish that he wouldn't get up to that kind of a thing."

'"Don't be such a little prig," I said; "if that's what they enjoy, just leave 'em to it."

'"I am making no moral judgement, Hyphen. I merely said that they – and my father – look unattractive when so engaged. I think Father got the idea from some murals in a villa he excavated in Thessaly. A coven of witches and warlocks in communal flagrance. He once explained to me that Thessaly was a great place for witches." "Still is," I told him; "but he wouldn't need to go that far to pick up the idea of orgies. It's quite common nearer home."

'Raisley and I were off to look at Roman remains in Provence, and of course there were plenty of orgies in some of the monuments round there, so I thought I'd better prepare him, to protect his aesthetic sensibilities from sudden shock. But in the end,' said Miss Jesty Hyphen, 'we never got round to the Roman bits. After two nights of sharing a room at Pau, and having to widdle in potties, as the lav was a furlong down the corridor, we cancelled the next night in our hotel and motored on towards Tarbes.

'"For God's sake, Hyphen," said little Raisley, "let's have proper rooms with our own baths and loos. The sight of you straddling a potty is more than I can stand." "You shouldn't have been looking." "No; and nor should *you*. Don't think I didn't spot you." "So now we both know what the other looks like," I said; "and no harm done." "If you say not, Hyphen; but from now on we'll have separate rooms, with our own private arrangements *en suite*, if you please."

'"We can't afford them," I said: "you know how small the currency allowance is." "I just happened to find four hundred pounds in my inside pocket," said Raisley: "We can change that."

'"Naughty, naughty," I said. "That's the only nice thing about still looking like a dear little ten year old," Raisley said; "one can get away with some handy smuggling." "I shouldn't play that trick too often, if I were you," I said: "a lot of excise men have nasty minds – and then watch out." "It's come off all right this time, Hyphen. So no more servants' bedrooms and tinkling chamber pots." "Righty. But where did you get the money in the first place?" "Daddy. Blackmail. 'I won't go,' I said to him – though of course I would have done, Hyphen, to be with you – 'I won't go and leave the coast clear unless you give me five hundred pounds.' 'Settle for four, boy?' 'Done.' 'A word of advice,' he said, handing over the cash: 'on your way from Bordeaux to the east, pop in at St-Bertrand-de-Comminges.' What about it, Hyphen?"

'"Why not?" I said. "There is nothing much in Tarbes.

And there's a three star hotel with a rosette for its food only a couple of miles from St-Bertrand, at Barbazan." So we booked in there, and the next morning we walked up the hill to the cathedral in St-Bertrand. We sat in the Cloister.

'"What's that?" he said; "on the lid of that sarcophagus?" (There were several of them strewn about.) "Latin," I said: "read it for yourself." "H . . . U . . . B . . . *Hubertus Breaze. Perfectus. Perfectus*, Hyphen?" "Old Cathar term," I told him: "a *perfectus* is a man who has forsworn the pleasures of the world and the flesh, and is therefore saved. But most Cathars postponed taking the oath till they were all but dead; they became 'perfect' just in time to escape hell-fire after a life of pleasure."

'This fascinated him. And he was still more fascinated when I told him that the Cathars postulated a Demiurge, or Creator, who was evil and had made the material world in order to tempt mankind away from the Good God. That was why one became "perfect", I told him: one renounced the world and the flesh in order to cleanse oneself of evil, which was the creation of the Demiurge or Devil. But of course that wasn't the end of it. As time went on, the Cathars conceived that the Devil or Demiurge wasn't just a fallen angel made and then damned by God, he was Satan, another and alternative God, a co-eternal and co-equal rival to the Good God, in perpetual conflict with him and (who knew?) perhaps destined to conquer him.

'"The pagan poets must have been on the side of the Demiurge," Raisley said, "though of course they couldn't have known that he'd later be called the Devil or Satan." "It's odd," I told him, "that this sarcophagus was a Cathar's. St-Bertrand wasn't really a centre of Catharism – though there are plenty of Cathar towns not far off."

"We'll go round them, Hyphen," he said: "we'll buy books and read about the Cathars and all their beliefs, from beginning to end. I love them, Hyphen. I want to see all their churches and all the places they lived in." Well, I thought, and why not? On the four hundred he'd lifted from Daddy we could live very comfortably (in those days) at the hotel in Barbazon, and every day we could go chugging off in my little Morris to see Cathar towns like Foix and Ax-les-Thermes and Tarascon (not the one near Arles but the one under the Pyrenees), charming places all of them, and then we might move east and set up headquarters in Narbonne . . . Roman remains in Provence are impressive but often stuffy, I thought, whereas the Cathar towns are rare and heady stuff, and if that's what interests him, lead him to it. After all, it was his daddy who'd started it all off by directing him to St-Bertrand.

'I loved that summer with Raisley Conyngham among the dead Cathars. True to his word, he read all the books, though some of them were long and in difficult French, and we discussed the whole history of the Albigensian Heresy from its inception in the mists of Gnosticism to the last Cathar survivors, a century and more after the Crusade of de Montfort which had been meant to wipe the sect out for ever. It was the later Cathars whom he really loved, because they were the ones that set up the full-blown dualism between God and the Demiurge, between God and Satan.

'"Either of 'em might win the match in the end, Hyphen," he said. "Right back at the beginning of the heresy all Cathars just sinned, and then repented, in order to become Perfects and be saved at the last moment. But later, much later, after de Montfort's Crusade, they decided they couldn't know which was the real God, the God or the Satan-cum-Demiurge-God; and so then they had to make a wager. Should they become Perfects as death came nearer, hoping that the Old God of Heaven was still the superior God and would be victorious, or should they go on enjoying the world and its delights, hoping to be saved by Satan when he conquered and crushed his enemies at the end of time? Or could they assume that this battle between God and Satan would go on for ever, so that being 'saved' was a mere matter of preference – for either you settled for Eternity in Heaven, or Eternity with the Devil/Demiurge among the flesh pots, in either case being cherished for; since neither of the Great Adversaries would ever overcome his enemy and destroy that enemy's followers, there could be no damnation either way, and Satan would care as kindly for his servants (albeit in a different fashion) as did God. Which would you have chosen, Hyphen?"'

The old woman went silent.

'Were there no more such summers?' said Piero.

'No,' said Jesty Hyphen sadly. 'In 1952 I was engaged to go on a tour of the Peloponnese, guiding and lecturing a large party. Raisley came too, but of course I was very preoccupied, and it was not the same. And then in 1953 he was ill. Some kind of infection of the chest which they thought might kill him. That was before we had antibiotics, you should remember, to keep the old and the feeble officiously alive. A simpler, saner, less crowded world.'

'In any case – antibiotics or no antibiotics – Raisley survived,' said Carmilla. 'A good thing, should you think? For Raisley himself? For the world at large?'

Miss Hyphen shrugged beneath her tartan rug.

'Your question is too large,' she said. 'All I know is that I had loved Raisley, in a sort, as we pottered about the foothills of the Pyrenees, raising ghosts and laying them. So I was anxious when he was ill, and gave thanks to whatever gods there be when he recovered and was strong enough to go on to Marcian College. I hoped there might be more holidays. Yet once he was at Marcian it seemed inappropriate that I should . . . intrude on him . . . with propositions for holidays. So I made none; and much to my sadness, neither did he.'

Fielding and Jeremy sought out Major Giles Glastonbury in his club.

'You do all the talking,' Jeremy said: 'you were in the Army with him.'

'A very long time ago.'

Giles Glastonbury stalked out of the Backgammon Room and took them upstairs to the Library.

'Glad to see you,' he said. 'Young Blockley was trying to cheat. Glad of an excuse to get clear before there was an embarrassing scene.'

'I thought,' said Jeremy, 'that no one cheated in places like this.'

'They used not to. Now they're brought up to think it's clever. Just as boys at Eton sometimes think it clever to talk in ugly townee accents. By emulating criminal or lower-class behaviour, they think they are keeping their options open, and proving that they are not what they themselves call "square". If only they knew how pathetic they look. They're too idle even to learn how to cheat properly – let alone to put in a bit of practice. They'd be merely laughable if they weren't such a nuisance. What can I do for you both?'

'Tell us about Raisley Conyngham and the Blue Mowbrays.'

There was a pause while Giles took this in. Fielding expected that he would at least ask why they were interested. However, after a few seconds Giles nodded to them as if he fully appreciated both the motive and the necessity for their curiosity, and began to pronounce on the topic:

'About the Blue Mowbrays there's nothing to tell. They were the rottenest regiment in the world, and now they're defunct.'

'How did they get their intriguing title?' Jeremy said.

'They started as a regiment privately raised in the late eighteenth century by a descendant of the great Mowbray. But the title was the only good thing they ever had, and that had been unofficially altered to the "Yellow Mowbrays" by the end of the Boer War. Horrible shower they were. And that's why Raisley Conyngham went to them. They were the only regiment that would have him.'

'There's some story,' said Fielding, 'that Raisley Conyngham was nearly found unfit to be commissioned anyway.'

'He was found unfit to be commissioned. He cracked up completely on some exercise in Dartmoor. He would have been chucked out of OCTU – and serve him right – if I hadn't managed to interfere from the War Box.'

'Why did you bother?'

'Because my cousin Prideau always said that Raisley would be a handy man to know some day. So I wanted him on my ledger . . . and here was a good way of putting him in the debtor column. Mind you, he'd tried to grease out of National Service altogether. He'd opted to go up to Cambridge first, hoping National Service would be done with by the time he finished. But it wasn't. So he pointed out to the Medical Board, quite truthfully, that he'd been very ill with his chest when he was seventeen. The Medical Board said he was now completely over that. Then he tried to get Doctor La Soeur to write him a certificate to exempt him. La Soeur would usually oblige for a hundred or two in that line, but he hated Raisley so much that he wouldn't oblige him at any price. So then

Raisley came to me and asked me if I could fix it. No, I said, I couldn't; but what I could do was to make it comfy for him: since he was a graduate, I could get him a National Service Commission inside four or five weeks (normally it would take as many months) from the day he joined – this by having him sent on some special short course for "senior recruits".

'This course was really intended to show the ropes to young scientists and the like whom the Army was in a hurry to commission; but Raisley had an excellent academic record and should therefore be qualified for commissioning in the same manner – at least if there was someone like me to give him a bit of a shove.

'Senior Officer Cadet Raisley Conyngham, provisionally accepted for one of the Carbineer regiments, started a one-month course on 1 June, 1956, with a view to an immediate commission at the end of it – provided that the result of his finals (still to be published) was satisfactory and that he completed his course in "the approved standard". In fact Raisley got a First (promulgated on 6 June), so that was very much all right, while "the approved standard" bit was, it was thought, a mere formality. But when Raisley started gibbering on an ordinary Night Exercise on Dartmoor (rather a soft one, to suit the nature of the course) this was obviously rather too bad . . . too bad even for a more or less fake course and even for the Carbineers. But luckily the Officer i/c the course was on my ledger to the extent of owing me a small favour, and he agreed to carry Raisley to the end of it if I could find a regiment to take him. So I did a deal with the Colonel Commandant of the Blue Mowbrays: if he would take Raisley as a Second Lieutenant, I would wangle the postponement of a pending enquiry into the illicit sale of the Blue Mowbrays' mess silver until they'd had time to rig the list a little and get in a few imitations.'

'And how,' said Fielding, 'did Raisley Conyngham's career in the Blue Mowbrays proceed?'

'Very commodiously. In return for an agreeable *douceur*, the constable of Brougham Castle Commanding the Regimental Donjon of the Blue Mowbrays (fancy name for the OC of the Regimental Depot in Cumberland) let Raisley off on unofficial leave for months at a time, and every now and again sent in a highly favourable personal report on him. Round the middle of 1958 Raisley was demobilized in the ordinary way. And that was it.'

'What did Conyngham do with all that leave?' Jeremy enquired.

'The gallant Constable of Brougham Castle neither knew nor cared – provided that Raisley kept himself well out of the way. He had to be warned, for example, that he was not to appear too prominently or too often on race courses: after all, if an officer spends six days a week for three months on the course, even though he would never conceivably appear in uniform, some nosy parker may discover who he is and decide to send a nasty note to the War House. But I remember the Constable's telling me what an easy and intelligent fellow Raisley was to deal with in matters like that. "Just goes off into France, leaving a Poste Restante address, some place called St-Girons or something of the sort, in case we have to call him back for anything," the Constable said: "not that we should call him back if we could possibly help it, but if there was a war or some rubbish he might be expected to take a bit of an interest . . . for whatever good it could do anyone." It occurred to me that I could now make a very stiff entry in Raisley's debit column: not only had I found him the cushiest way to a commission and rescued the silly sod when he fucked it up, I'd also found him a totally sympathetic regiment which would let him do exactly what suited him, for all the world like a young grandee in the piping days of Fitzroy Somerset.'

'Interesting, all that,' said Jeremy, as Fielding and he made their way towards Wilton's for dinner; 'but I don't know that we've heard much to our purpose.'

'Glastonbury might have asked us to dine with him,' grouched Fielding: 'after all, I was in his Squadron. His Second-in-Command at that.'

'We'll do much better at Wilton's than at any club, even that upper-class sanctuary of Giles's.'

'How do you know?' grated Fielding. 'You don't belong to any clubs. And you won't, after that squalid fiasco in Australia. What do you know about the food in clubs?'

'All right,' said Jeremy equably, 'shall we dine at yours? The Thackeray, isn't it?'

'No. Wilton's.'

'It'll cost four times as much as the Thackeray.'

'It'll be four times better,' said Fielding; 'and you're so rich you can pay for both of us.'

'All right,' said Jeremy. 'No need for hints – even one as delicate and subtle as that. I should have paid anyway.'

'Sorry,' said Fielding, feeling rather grimy: 'what was that you said about how we didn't hear anything to our purpose from Giles?'

'Just that. That we heard nothing to our purpose.'

'But we did. St-Girons. That's the place which the Constable told Giles that Raisley gave as his Poste Restante address.'

'"St-Girons or something of the sort", as I remember.'

'Military *façon de parler*,' Fielding said. 'Regular officers learn very early in their careers never to be too precise in stating details in case someone blames them if they've got it wrong. St-Girons. Forget "the something of the sort". St-Girons – a totally unimportant place but with

92

a rather memorable and charming name. That's why it stuck in the Constable's head. And in Giles's as well, for all these years.'

'And what if it did?'

'Come, Jeremy. St-Girons is not far from St-Bertrand-de-Comminges and Barbazon. The inference is clear. Raisley had remembered his summer holiday with his old chum, Hyphen, and was spending his leave – months and months of it, we hear – going over the ground again.'

Carmilla and Piero decided that the best way they could tackle Ullacote was simply to go there accompanied by Auntie Flo, who had been an old racing crony of Raisley Conyngham and could therefore announce, without impropriety, that she had been passing through Timber-scombe with her friends and had taken the opportunity to call. Only the plot was that she would not be announcing this to Raisley himself, who was back at school teaching, but to whomsoever happened to be taking care of the place in his absence. It would be interesting to establish who, at present, this was, and what sort of state the house and stables were now in; and they could at least hope (on the strength of Auntie Flo's taste for racing) for a good look at the horses.

'Raisley's Private Trainer,' said Auntie Flo, as they all set out from Sandy Lodge (HQ for the operation), 'used to be a pathetic drunk called Jack Lamprey, who, how-ever, was a marvellous hand with the horses. But now Jack is dead, and Gat-Toothed Jenny, his Head Lass, has gone away, and God alone knows who'll be there.'

The answer was chilling. They were greeted by Abel Thynne, a former Head Lad, whom Raisley Conyngham had kept in his employment, until now he was well past three score years and ten, because he (Raisley) believed in rewarding loyal service. Abel remembered Auntie Flo from race meetings long ago and was happy to show them whatever they wanted to see. The house itself was in tolerable condition, kept up by a Scottish couple who minded their business and nobody else's, under the nominal supervision of Abel, who had advanced with the years to the status of Honorary Factor. The stables, however, were desolate. The deserted stalls dripped and gaped: the yard was fouled by plastic bags and broken bottles: even the bell had been borne away, by one of the departing stable lads. For all the lads and lassies had gone now; the horses, they were told by Abel, had been sent for keeping to Prideau Glastonbury in Herefordshire, where the stallion, Lover Pie, who had been Master Marius Stern's favourite when he worked there briefly the previous spring, was sick nearly to death. There were no plans for bringing any of the horses back to Ullacote. 'If only Miss Jenny would return,' said Abel; 'but she is now in service to my Lord Canteloupe in Wiltshire, and he will make her a kind master for all his proud ways.'

'God, how depressing,' said Auntie Flo, as they drove back along the coast road from Minehead to Bridgwater and Burnham. 'Poor old Abel. Nothing to do but die. The heart has gone out of the place. Whatever you may think of Raisley, up to the end of last summer he kept some beautiful hurdlers and steeplechasers.'

'I think an ill wind is blowing over Ullacote,' said Piero Caspar. 'Sicilians have a keen nose for an ill wind.'

'If Raisley smells it he may turn vengeful,' said Carmilla.

'He must have smelt it by now.'

'Perhaps,' said Carmilla, 'we may find the germ of his revenge in what Fielding was telling us, that Raisley had persuaded Marius "to keep his options open" and not to tell Tessa that they are in fact half-brother and -sister.'

'There can only be an evil connection between Marius

and Tessa,' said Piero, 'if Marius is required to go again to your sister. For if he goes, Tessa will be there with her; and then – '

' – I think it will be some time before it is decided,' said Carmilla, 'decided, that is, whether Thea is to be submitted to child-bearing again. A lot will depend on whether Canteloupe likes the baby girl of which Flo delivered her at the New Year. If he does, he may abandon the idea of having a son manufactured for him.'

'Meanwhile,' said Piero, 'if we are to fight Raisley Conyngham, we need to know wherein he is strong and wherein he is vulnerable. As you have said, Carmilla, the clue may lie in the Languedoc.'

'Why?' Carmilla said.

'That was your feeling, you said.'

'I'm not sure it was well based. Just an early impression, which I was perhaps too quick to pass on.'

'An early impression, I dare say,' said Piero, 'but one that has surely been reinforced since we have learned of his obsession with that terrain . . . as reported to you and me by Miss Jesty Hyphen in her account of the summer they spent there together among the dead Cathars.'

'That summer was a long time ago,' Carmilla said.

'Obsessions linger a long time, Miss Carmilla.'

'Granted. We shall still need to know much more than we know yet before we can start seeking for his secrets in the Languedoc with any confidence. Now, that curious figure, his father – should we not try to find out more about him?'

'A *flaneur*. And an antiquary who in fact prompted Raisley's interest in St-Bertrand-de-Comminges . . . but casually and almost *en passant*. I do not think any investigation of the father will help us further.'

'Possibly not,' said Carmilla. 'But I shall wish to learn much more than I've learned yet about Raisley's interest in the Languedoc before I shall be happy to start trying to find a scent there.'

'And yet a few days ago you seemed practically certain.'

'A first impression, as I've just said. I now wish to be much better informed before I commit our time and energy – and money – in that quarter. After all . . . I am meant to be writing a book.'

'We all look foward to it,' said Auntie Flo. 'Marius was talking to me about it only the other day – he is very intrigued by your subject. I only hope he is still here to enjoy it when it is published.'

'Come, come,' said Carmilla. 'Raisley may be a threat to Marius, a moral threat, in the long term. But you sound as if you expect him to drag Marius down into hell-fire at any moment – like the devils and Don Juan.'

'Something of the kind,' said Auntie Flo; 'not quite so theatrical, perhaps, but just as final. You seem to be losing your urgency in this matter, Carmilla. As I under-stand it, it was you who first organized the hunt.'

'And convened the huntsmen in my house,' added Piero.

'You make me seem like Artemis.'

'Yes.

> Thou that makest day of night,
> Goddess, excellently bright.

Our guide, our leader,' said Piero. 'Our light, our hope.'

'Please keep this thing in proper perspective, Piero. Of course we must follow where the clues lead; but there is no need to be precipitant – to be childish and hysterical.'

'Raisley Conyngham,' said Auntie Flo, 'is and has long been a rich man, as the Apocrypha has it, "furnished with ability". He is efficient, competent, commanding when he needs to be. Why do you think he has allowed his stable to sink, almost overnight, into ruin? Do you really suppose he could not have prevented this? That it has been brought about by an ill wind against which he is powerless?'

Piero and Carmilla were silent now. The old woman, sitting in the co-driver's seat, turned on them both. It was as though her mouth stretched the entire width of her face, one half of it speaking to Carmilla, to whom she now presented her left profile, the other half, separately, to Piero in the back, towards whom her right profile thrust and stabbed from her twisted neck.

'Don't you understand?' she screeched. 'The ill wind comes from Raisley himself. He has cursed his stable, part of his own possessions, in order that the curse may spread to those that worked and were happy there. "The Bailey has borne the bell away." The curse has claimed that poor sot Jack already. The gallant stallion, Lover Pie, is dying, so Abel tells us. And when will it claim Marius, who was happy there, grooming Lover Pie, in the spring?'

After a time, Carmilla said in a small voice:

'Surely . . . it is Raisley's wish to possess and use Marius, not to curse him?'

'Possess? Use? Curse? Where is the difference, Carmilla? If Raisley wishes to do the first and the second, why should he balk at the third? Perhaps he must do the third to prove his power and make it total.'

Not wishing to disturb Tessa or Marius by obtruding themselves on the school, or (for that matter) to risk the anger or curiosity of Raisley Conyngham, Fielding and Jeremy had decided to conduct their enquiries through Jeremy's father, Lord Luffham of Whereham (Peter Morrison as had been) who had been a governor of the school for some years now and had lately been honoured by enthronement and 'gowning' before the Masters and the Sixth Form.

'Since you ask,' said Luffham, sitting at dinner under Orpen's portrait of his father, 'I have never heard anything against Raisley Conyngham. He has the name of a brilliant teacher, and there has been no breath of scandal against him in all my time as a governor.'

'But you didn't like him when you met him at your "gowning", Father,' Jeremy said.

'No. I thought him specious and mannered. I think he is too rich for his position. A teacher of the classics has no business owning race horses.'

They were interrupted by the 'Chamberlain', an old family servant.

'I have just thought, my lord,' said the Chamberlain to Lord Luffham of Whereham, 'that since you have ceded the property to Master Jeremy and are here only by his invitation, Master Jeremy should sit at the head of the table, where you are now, and you should sit under the portrait of your late wife, where he is now. Would you like me to change your places?'

'You must not interrupt, Chamberlain,' said Jeremy calmly, 'or I shall have to ask you to leave the room. My father and I prefer to sit as we are.'

Deeply hurt, the Chamberlain came from 'at ease' to 'attention' in his position against the wall.

'Did you ever hear anything,' said Fielding to Luffham, 'of Conyngham's sabbatical year?'

'Plenty,' said Luffham. 'I was against it. But most of my colleagues considered that Marcian College was honouring Conyngham, and through Conyngham the school, by offering to assist his research. So I let them have their way. If I remember rightly, Conyngham was released from May '75 to September '76 . . . without pay but without loss of place or seniority. A very long time, I should have thought, for a mature man to waste on a mere piece of academic research.'

'Come, Peter,' said Fielding: 'let's not be philistine about this.'

'Very well, Fielding. Let us not be philistine,' said Luffham of Whereham. 'Let us just say that no one on the Governing Body had any very clear idea of what this research was about, that at the end of the fifteen months off which he spent on it we are still no clearer, and that after a further six years not one word of it has been published.'

'That is what happens with research,' said Jeremy. 'It is very seldom published, and then only after many years, and more often than not it is never even done at all.'

'Mr Raisley Conyngham did his all right,' said the Chamberlain from the wall.

'What do you know about it, Chamberlain?' Jeremy said.

'Since I've been told by you not to interrupt, Master Jeremy,' said the Chamberlain pettishly, 'I had better hold my tongue.'

'You have already interrupted. What do you know about Conyngham's research? What could you possibly know?'

'I was Lord Canteloupe's servant, sir, as you may know, when he was still plain Captain Detterling of Hamilton's Horse.'

'Yes, we do know. What has that to do with it?'

'Captain Detterling does not forget old companions, sir. He writes from time to time. So does his friend, Major Glastonbury. We was all three in India, you see, me as the servant, when Captain Detterling and Major Glastonbury (Lieutenant-Colonel 'e was then, just for a time) were working in Intelligence just after the war.'*

* *Sound the Retreat* by S. R. (Blond & Briggs, 1971)

'The less said about all *that* the better for all concerned,' said Luffham, smiling slyly. 'Not a wholesome period in British History.'

'I dare say not, my lord. What I'm leading up to is that Major Glastonbury has a cousin called Prideau Glastonbury who was at Cambridge with Mr Raisley Conyngham; and so Major Glastonbury came to know Mr Conyngham along of his cousin Prideau. Well, some years ago, 1975, Major Glastonbury sent me a Christmas card. Regimental card it was, though of course the poor old bloody regiment was long dead by then, with the old Skull and Crossbones on the front and inside a print of some young buck in the mess kit worn in the year of Waterloo. Anyway, Major Glastonbury had put two cards in the envelope by mistake. The first said "To the Great Teetotaller" – that was what Captain Detterling and he used to call me because I never drank – and was, of course, for me. The second said "To Raisley with Best Wishes for your grave crawl under the Pyrenees. Seriously, you cunning bastard, if you do come up with anything worthwhile, don't waste it. Black Tombs can spew Red Gold – but not on the academic market. G.G."'

'What did you do with that card, Corporal?' said Fielding, using the rank the man had carried as Detterling's servant, the time when Fielding had known him best.

'Kept it, Major Fielding. Otherwise I'd never have remembered all that, now would I? I like to look at my Christmas cards from old friends from time to time, and though that one wasn't strictly for me, I've always enjoyed it. Poetic, you see. Black Tombs can spew Red Gold – I often wonder what the Major meant.'

'Whatever Major Glastonbury meant,' said Carmilla to Fielding Gray, Jeremy Morrison and Piero Caspar in her

100

rooms in Lancaster College, Cambridge (where she had called a meeting to decide on future action), 'I still can't be confident that it warrants a journey to the Languedoc. It was a flippant message – a joke.'

'To Giles Glastonbury,' said Fielding, 'everything was a joke.'

'I simply don't trust it,' Carmilla said. ' "Black Tombs can spew Red Gold." Night Nursery stuff – a Tale at Bedtime.'

'I simply adore it,' said Piero. 'But then we Sicilians take Night Nursery stuff more seriously than you Anglo-Saxons.'

'*You* didn't have a Night Nursery,' said Jeremy in a rather malicious way (one queen putting down another), 'in your family hutch in the slums of Syracuse.'

'But we had plenty of stories at bedtime,' Piero said. 'People crowding round one's little cradle – a handy fruit box – to tell tales and give one a tickle.'

'Frivolous,' said Carmilla. 'You're not serious.'

'Oh, but I am,' Piero said. 'We combine the frivolous with the serious in a way that you, Miss Carmilla, would never understand. In Sicily a hideous history of emasculation, for example, is seldom told to one without a tweak of one's little penis. Ghosts, to take another example: they are eminently comic as well as horrible, so we combine horror and comedy in telling of them. Or look at the catacombs in Palermo: full of grand, purple cardinals hanging grotesquely from hooks.'

'That Christmas card does at least suggest a line on Raisley,' said Fielding. 'Jeremy's father was no help – he was adamant on the man's respectability and pooh-poohed everything to do with his research; but this sabbatical year as described by Glastonbury – "a grave crawl under the Pyrenees", a search for the "Red Gold" which may be spewed forth by "Black Tombs" – it does suggest an exciting and mysterious journey into hidden places; it does convey a whiff of simmering lava.'

'What does Jeremy say?' said Carmilla: 'Jeremy, the man of bardic vision, the man who was briefly Virgil.'

'Don't mock,' Jeremy said.

Carmilla winced but did not apologize. 'What do you think of this trail?' she said.

'You say,' said Jeremy, 'that Miss Jesty Hyphen was full of Raisley's passion for Cathars in 1951. We also know Raisley went again into Cathar country, for months at a time while on bought and illicit furlough from the Depot of the Blue Mowbrays between 1956 and 1958. And yet again, we know that he went once more in 1975 and stayed until the spring or summer of 1976. What puzzles me is why he didn't go at all for nearly twenty years, between leaving the Blue Mowbrays and taking his sabbatical leave from the school.'

'It was obviously,' said Carmilla, 'an adolescent infatuation which faded – and then returned, as adolescent infatuations sometimes do, many years later, only to die out once more without benefit of recorded research.'

'Not yet recorded,' Jeremy said; 'perhaps suppressed for good reason. Nor do we know for certain that the infatuation is dead. If we went to the Languedoc, to all Raisley's places –'

'We don't know which they are,' Carmilla put in.

'We know the names of those told to you and Piero by Jesty Hyphen. If we started examining these places, and if Raisley heard of it, then, knowing or strongly suspecting that we are his enemies and mean him no good, he might feel that he should revisit his old territory to guard or to conceal.'

'He might,' Carmilla said. 'He couldn't go there until the end of the school Quarter in March.'

'He could always take sabbatical leave again if he

thought it was really urgent. Despite the desolation of his stables, he is still, as old Flo remarked, a rich man. Now then: if he *didn't* take a sabbatical and follow us, we should have a clear run in a clear country, casting about for whatever might help us. If he *did* come, we could concentrate on observing him (while he was observing us), and the results might be very informative. Either way the thing could be intriguing.'

'A vote,' said Carmilla. 'Those in favour of going to France now, without further investigation.'

Three hands rose.

'Those against,' said Carmilla, and raised her own.

'Yet you were the first to suggest the Languedoc as a likely hunting ground,' said Fielding, 'at that opening conference in the fens.'

'As I say, I have had doubts since then,' Carmilla said. 'But of course I shall come too. The fascination of the hunt, you see. Always absorbing, even if one is on a false scent. I know we shouldn't start just yet, I know we should try to gather more evidence first, I know that you are just being silly and wishful, but I simply can't resist it. I think, too, that we should remember the plea for greater urgency which Auntie Flo made the other day. Her talk of a "curse" may not be easily credible – certainly not to me – but it does not do to be blasé when old women utter as fiercely as she did. I am sure,' Carmilla said to Piero, 'that all Sicilians would agree with me there.'

'But what about that book of yours?' said Piero. '*A History of Medieval Diseases*. There will now ensue a sad delay. The learned world will be disappointed, your reputation as a diligent scholar will be eroded – '

' – The learned world will be patient a little longer, I fancy. As for my reputation,' said Carmilla, 'I can afford a little set-back and delay. Like Raisley Conyngham, I am rich.'

'You are all rich except me,' said Fielding. 'I only hope you will raise a purse for my expenses.'

Gat-Toothed Jenny, knocking a ball about in Canteloupe's Fives court (of course she had permission), sent it from the back with her left hand high on to the front wall. It would bounce up on the step. As she mounted the step to continue her solitary rally, she tripped and was flung sideways against the corner of the buttress, which (so fast was she falling) sliced right into her scalp like an axe. When Leonard Percival, Canteloupe's decrepit but perpetually prying Private Secretary, spotted her and her blood under the buttress fifteen minutes later and limped away like Lazarus to raise the alarm, she was not yet dead but might just as well have been.

Old mortality tolled from the Campanile, one bell only, cracked. The coffin, borne shoulder-high by six of Canteloupe's yeoman tenants, floated steadily across the Great Court, past the Fives court, and towards the Grave Ground, which was in a far corner of the Rose Garden.

'She was a good girl, Jenny,' said Canteloupe to Giles Glastonbury, as they walked behind the coffin: 'why not bury her with the family, I thought? She's no people of her own. Come to that, what are you doing here?'

'I knew her a bit when she was still with Raisley Conyngham,' Glastonbury said: 'a good girl, as you say. She was kind to Jack Lamprey.'

'Particularly just at the end,' Canteloupe said. 'She was kind to Marius too.'

'Does he know she's dead?'

'Yes. Not much interested, to judge from the note he sent. Tessa, on the other hand – she wanted to come to the funeral. I had to tell her,' said Canteloupe, 'that the custom here is to ban women from funerals. Burying is men's work.'

'Poor Jenny,' said Giles Glastonbury as they stood by the hole, the coffin poised over it.

'Well out of it, I'd say: there wasn't going to be much in anything for her.'

'She loved her horses,' said Giles, 'those she took care of for other people. What are you going to do with yours?'

'Send 'em to your cousin Prideau, like Raisley did with his. Sell 'em later. The accountants have been stroppy.'

'Funds sinking?'

'Cant-Fun isn't doing what it ought to.'

'Cant-Fun?'

'Trade name,' said Canteloupe. 'Trade name for, among other more cultural public entertainments, the Cock, Cunt and Cola Circus which I run for the sweaty nightcaps.' He gestured across the hole and towards the hedge. 'Other side of those yews, but you can't hear or smell it because Balbo Blakeney designed the thing so that the house and garden should be prole-proof. It used to make a packet, Cant-Fun did, but it's been going downhill. No reason why – Henry Bath at Longleat is doing better than ever. But something about this place seems to be putting people off.'

'Perhaps that cracked bell bothers them. Can't you do something about it?'

'Never get another bell like that. Old Mortality. Never get it mended – no craftsmen these days. Never mind. Its message is all the clearer for the crack.'

'It's not a message people want to hear.'

Gat-Toothed Jenny, at least, wouldn't hear it any more, under the earth that rattled on to her box.

'I have something to consult you about,' said Giles to Canteloupe as they walked back across the Rose Garden: 'Raisley Conyngham.'

105

'What about the brute?'

'Your sister-in-law, Carmilla Salinger,' said Giles, 'is out to finish him. I had Fielding Gray and Jeremy Morrison infesting my club the other day and asking about Raisley's time in the Blue Mowbrays, clearly with uncharitable intent.'

'Why should that have anything to do with Carmilla?' Canteloupe said.

'She sent them. Fielding took notes of what I told them. He put 'em in an envelope and addressed it to Carmilla at Lancaster.'

'You saw this address?'

'Later, when he'd gone. He left the envelope behind.'

'He *what*?' said Canteloupe.

'He didn't put it properly into his pocket. It must have got stuck half-way in – probably in the ticket pocket at the side.'

'Fielding wants to take a grip of himself.'

'We all do at our age. Anyway, there it was on the sofa after he'd gone. I noticed Carmilla's address, then opened it. It confirmed some meeting in Cambridge for a day or two later, then gave a precis of what I'd told him and Jeremy.'

'And what had you told them?'

'The truth,' said Giles; 'why not? Those two buggers are clever and persistent, and if I hadn't told them, sooner or later somebody else would. So I told 'em how Raisley spent most of his military service on leave, and gave some address in the Foix region in case he was wanted to have tea in the Depot with the Queen. If, as I think, they're enquiring seriously – '

'They certainly will be if Carmilla's behind it – '

'Then they'll know he went off to the same area in 1975 and '76, about twenty years later. They will conclude that

Raisley Conyngham is interested in the terrain just north of the Pyrenees. They may even go there.'

'Bad for Raisley?' said Canteloupe.

'Not at all. They'll be on Raisley's ground. He knows it, they don't. So he can play will-o'-the-wisp, and entice them into the marshes to sink without trace . . . unless they get really clever and win against the odds, and Raisley ends up in the bog. Good result either way,' opined Giles Glastonbury.

'Spell it out to me,' said Canteloupe. 'I never trust these we-win-either-way situations.'

'Well, as far as you're concerned,' said Giles Glastonbury, 'indeed as far as we're both concerned, the trouble with Raisley Conyngham is that he knows just too much. He knows, for example, that Marius Stern is Nausikaa's father – and that Marius may go again to Thea if you want a son.'

'That's out,' said Canteloupe; 'I'm settling for Nausikaa. She's lovely, you know. Lady Nausikaa Sarum, to be Baroness Sarum of Old Sarum when I die. I want no more of Marius in my lady's chamber. Let her and little Tessa have it to themselves in peace. That way Thea will be happy.'

'Good decision. The fact remains that Marius is the real father of Nausikaa. Therefore we want Raisley silent. Therefore we want him *either* to win in any contest with Carmilla, so that he's in a generous temper and not about to spill any of your personal beans for spite; *or* we want him dead, having been, as I say, decoyed by Carmilla & Co into one of his own pet bogs in the Comté de Foix or thereabouts.'

'The trouble is,' said Canteloupe, 'that even if he is decoyed into one of his own pet bogs he won't necessarily vanish for ever in a vortex of bubbles. He may work his way out again, covered in slime and stink and feeling mean enough to spill all the beans in the tin – including the reprehensible truth about poor little Tully's demise.'*

'Not,' said Giles, 'if we make it plain to him from the start that we're on his side, and give him all the help we can. Now then: it is clear that Carmilla wants him disgraced and out of the way because she's jealous of his influence over Marius. But she won't want him dead – because Carmilla don't approve of killing people. Raisley disgraced but still alive could be very dangerous to us, as I've just been saying. But if we help him with a few timely tips now, and hang about with a mobile bath unit, so to speak, to cleanse and comfort him if he ends up in the shit, then Raisley will be happy to keep in with us and will not, therefore, promulgate nasty tales about the genesis of Nausikaa or the decease of Tully Sarum.'

'You could be right,' Canteloupe said.

'So I shall now go to Raisley,' said Giles as they passed the Fives court, in one wall of which, he noticed, a tablet had now been affixed to record the death of Gat-Toothed Jenny, 'sturdy, loyal and amiable, who played in this Court and fell one day, entering Black Hades. May Persephone ease the passage of this lady through the realm of Dis and bring her where her friends abide.' 'I shall now go to Raisley,' said Giles when he had read Jenny's epitaph (as good as any, he supposed), 'and tell him what is in the troubled air. I think that we have more to gain with him than against him – as long as he still breathes.'

Giles Glastonbury and Raisley Conyngham had agreed to meet in the paddock of the race course at Regis Priory, a few days after Giles's conversation with Canteloupe at Gat-Toothed Jenny's funeral.

* See *New Seed for Old* by S. R. (Muller, 1987 or GraftonBooks)

'A long way from your school,' said Giles. 'I was rather surprised you found the arrangement suitable.'

'I'm at Ullacote for a few days. Not too far from here. The school is having its Valentine's Exit.'

'How are things at Ullacote?'

'Bad,' said Raisley Conyngham complacently. 'As you probably know, all the horses have been sent to your cousin Prideau. The stalls are rotting. The house will last a while, but I shan't be going there much myself, still less inviting anybody.'

'But only a few months ago . . . last spring . . . everything was so pleasant there. Stables spick and span and run as tight as a man-o'-war; healthy horses; smiling, rosy servants.'

'That,' said Raisley Conyngham, 'was when Marius Stern and Teresa Malcolm were there. And Jack Lamprey, and Jenny the Stable Lass. Now they are all gone, Giles; two of 'em to Tartarus.'

'I should have thought that Jack and Jenny had deserved better than Tartarus. The Elysian Fields for them, I should have thought.'

'Would you?' said Conyngham. 'There are one or two things which you don't know. Nor am I going to tell you, Giles; not yet. But I will just tell you that nothing in any of this is quite what it seems.'

'No? Thank you for the tip,' said Giles.

A bell rang and the jockeys started to mount.

'I see there's a horse of Prideau's running,' Raisley Conyngham said. 'Where's Prideau this afternoon?'

'Sulking, I expect. He's never been the same since his son died. I think he blames you. There's some story that you deliberately infected the boy.'

'Nothing in any of this is quite what it seems,' Raisley repeated.

A thin, malignant sleet began to fall. Raisley and Giles

109

moved under the trees. The horses and their jockeys filed patiently out on to the course.

'Carmilla Salinger's after you,' said Giles. 'She wants you arraigned and exiled – exiled for life.'

'I suspected as much. She and that interfering old woman from Burnham-on-Sea called at Ullacote a while ago. Prying.'

'Fielding Gray and Jeremy Morrison have been asking questions. They came to my club.'

'None of this surprises me in the least.'

'So you know the lot already,' said Giles. 'No need for this meeting. I apologize for suggesting it.'

'Not at all. This is a favourite course of mine. That jockey up on Prideau's horse, Mercury,' said Raisley Conyngham: 'Danny Chead. I don't like the look of him.'

'Nobody does. Oddly enough, his father was Corporal-Major in the 10th Sabre Squadron when I commanded. He hates Danny. He prays every night, he once told me, that the boy will fall and break his neck.'

The two men started to walk through the sleet to the Stand. Giles led the way through a gate marked 'Stewards Only'.

'You're not a Steward today, surely?' Raisley Conyngham said.

'No. But you'll find none of them will object to us. I want a word with Dorchester about those rails. They should have been taken away several years ago – as he promised me they would be.'

'Nasty spikes. Almost as bad as Folkestone. But they've got some of those plastic rails some yards out on the course itself.'

'The spiked rails should have gone years ago,' said Glastonbury, 'and everybody knows it.'

'Another thing about Carmilla Salinger and her crowd,' said Raisley. 'I had a letter from my old classics mistress,

Jesty Hyphen. They've been down to the south coast to question her.'

'What does she know?' said Giles.

Raisley noticed that all the Stewards drew away from Giles and himself, though none objected orally to their presence. The starter sent off the seventeen-horse field towards the first of the nine hurdles.

'Jesty Hyphen,' said Raisley, 'took me to the Pyrenees one summer. It was with her I first got interested in the area: Cathar country. Danny Chead is pulling Mercury fit to take his head off. Hyphen couldn't have told them much, except that we had a very agreeable and scholarly excursion.'

'But suppose they know that you've been going there for long periods since?'

'They'll discover nothing to their purpose, even if they go there themselves and look under every blade of grass with a microscope . . . unless I give 'em a few clues.' He shook his head, as if to dispute Carmilla's competence when it came to peering under blades of grass, then suddenly looked slightly sad, an expression Giles had never seen on his face before. 'Poor old Hyphen,' said Raisley Conyngham, and shook his head again. 'A shrewd, kind woman. But she fancied just a drop too much in the evenings. They had to make her retire from Brydales early – not because of the tipple but because of a fuss got up by blacks. There weren't any nogs worth talking of at Brydales until about 1960, and if there were they didn't read classics. But later on, when all those black Ambassadors started coming to London, a lot of them sent their spawn to Brydales – including a fellow called Cham Koreoti from Nigeria, who'd read classics at Cambridge (very unusual) at about my time and Prideau's. He wanted his son to do the same. He'd heard great things of Jesty Hyphen – who rose to the occasion, overcame her mild distaste for Africans, and taught the Koreoti boy (Sitrep) for all she was worth . . . and got him an Exhibition at his father's old college, Corpus Christi.'

'Good going,' said Giles, who had never met Jesty Hyphen and was not very interested in this story.

'So one would have thought. But Cham Koreoti said his *mtoto* should have got a Foundation Scholarship. He blamed Jesty for not giving him enough attention, and altogether got up such a rumpus (although the boy, Sitrep, stood up for Jesty and said she'd given him hours of extra tuition) that the wet and worthy Governors of Brydales backed down and sacked her, in their unctuous deference to negritude – at the same time passing clandestine money under her skirt and into her knickers (so to speak) to stop her making a case of it and to keep her in comfort for the rest of her life. I'll tell you what, Giles: there's something the matter with Danny Chead. His face is like a skull – and that horse Mercury doesn't mean to be held back any longer.'

'What will you do,' said Giles Glastonbury, 'now you know that Carmilla's after you?'

'Wait and see what she does. No one's got anything against me at the school or anywhere else. But if she does turn ugly I rather think . . . that one bad turn deserves another.'

'You mean, if she tries anything you'll hit back. What with?'

'Ah. You're afraid I may tell tales about her sister, Theodosia,' said Raisley. 'Certainly not. That might damage Canteloupe – and possibly Marius. Theodosia and her husband are safe from any delation on my part, Giles. If I go for Carmilla, it will be just for her and her gang. I don't suppose you mind much what happens to them?'

112

'Not to Caspar or Morrison,' said Giles Glastonbury; 'but I've always had a soft spot for Fielding Gray. He was my second-in-command in the old days – when Danny Chead's old man was Corporal-Major.'

'I'll bear that in mind, Giles, should I be compelled to take action.'

'Take action . . . with intent to do what?'

'I've just told you. It remains to be seen. Let them start the game, if they must. Danny Chead and that gelding are hating each other.'

With two furlongs to run and one hurdle to jump, Mercury was pressing to the front of the field, despite being hauled back by Danny Chead, who was straining to his work with both hands like a fisherman with a corpse on his hook. Over the last hurdle they went, Mercury squirming in his efforts to break free. A furlong to run. Mercury swerved right, reared, twisted violently, and flung Danny over the white plastic rail to land, supine, on the first of the spiked rails beyond.

'Pity the Corporal-Major's not here,' observed Giles; 'he'd have enjoyed that. And now, Dorchester,' he called along the Steward's Box, 'you're going to have to explain why you didn't keep your promise about removing those rails.'

'Too costly,' grated Dorchester from under his *homme-qui-rît* moustache; 'just as simple as that. I doubt whether anyone's going to raise much of a row about that little turd, Danny Chead. All the other jockeys hate him.'

'To say nothing of his own father. Still . . . they may feel that there but for the grace of God or the Devil go they – lying on the top of that fence with two spikes between their shoulder blades.' The two deep, dark clefts between Glastonbury's nostrils and the corners of his mouth quivered and rippled, though whether with indignation or amusement Raisley could not tell. 'Anyway,'

113

Giles went on to Dorchester, 'there'll be a spinechilling shriek from the senior nannies in the Jockey Club.'

'Don't you believe it, Giles. Danny's got away with hundreds of filthy jobs. They'll be glad to see an end of him.'

'It's those spikes that are going to be complained of, Dorchester, not the damage to Danny Chead.'

'Troublesome time the ambulance men are having . . . trying to lift him off. Good job the spikes ain't barbed. But nobody's going to complain of them, Giles. You know why not? Bit of local history. A couple of Hun bomber pilots, shot down on the way back from Bristol, split themselves arse to tit on those spikes in 1942.'

'I never heard that before.'

'Did you not? The press releases just going out will remedy your ignorance, and everybody else's. By tonight it will be all over the West Country, and by tomorrow the whole kingdom. You couldn't have expected us to dismantle a museum piece, hallowed by its association with the People's War for Freedom, now could you?'

Isobel Stern and her friend, Jo-Jo Guiscard, stood on the south side of the cloister of the cathedral of St-Bertrand-de-Comminges and looked down on to a meadow below, where Jo-Jo's husband, Jean-Marie, was picking grass and putting it into a briefcase.

'This new theory of Jean-Marie's,' said Jo-Jo, 'that Cathar "perfects" in the early period of Albigensianism fed off grass, is going to lead to tears.'

'Why on earth should it?'

'He's going to ask us to try it out and see how we feel. It is our duty, he is going to say, to help him with the research for his book.'

'Grass will be a monotonous diet,' said Isobel, 'but it

will have the merit of economy. Perhaps he would allow us to vary it a little with a few nettles and wild flowers.'

'Daddy says the Cathars wouldn't eat flowers,' said three-year-old Oenone, who was amusing herself by riding astride a chunky corbel which jutted low from the west wall of the cloister. 'They wouldn't eat them because they were so pretty that they were sinful. Daddy says the Cathars hated pretty things because they came from the Devil.'

'Interesting,' said Isobel. 'Of course all Cathars believed that the physical world was created by the Devil as Demiurge, but to the early ones the Devil really was still the Devil and not an Alternative God. So I suppose the "perfects" or "parfaits" might have forced themselves only to eat grass – the dullest food that grows.'

'When Daddy and I were picking grass yesterday,' said Oenone, 'he told me that there were different kinds of it. That is why he is putting it in his briefcase. It has things fitted into it to separate the different kinds of grass.'

'He talks to her the whole time when they go on their expeditions,' said Jo-Jo.

'Very good for her education.'

'She gets bored with it sometimes. That is why she is not down there with him now. No question of it, Isobel: if Oenone is to be properly educated, she must be sent back to England.'

'Not just yet, I think. Let's see now: what news from Blighty?'

Isobel plumped her splendid bum on to a closed sarcophagus and started opening the letters which she had just collected from the Poste Restante.

'Item,' she said: 'I have an obscenely large sum of money which has accumulated in my Deposit Account.'

'Why not have some fun with it? Or give some of it away?'

'That is not how money should be used,' Isobel said. 'It is not to be frittered away on frivolous pleasure, neither is it to be scattered down the wind to scavengers.'

'Then what should one do with it?'

'Suppress it,' said Isobel. 'Lock it away. If it is let loose, it only makes trouble. It gives rise to envy, hatred, and violence, both physical and moral.'

'If you have so much money,' said Oenone to Isobel, 'will you please buy Oenone an ice-lolly.'

'Don't push her too hard,' Jo-Jo said.

'Item,' said Isobel: 'Marius' O levels are at last to take place; in March.'

'Has Marius written?'

'No. My son no longer writes to me. His sister Rosie has sent this news.'

'When Rosie was here at Christmas, she said Marius had been neglecting his work,' Oenone said. 'She sounded quite cross.'

'Item,' said Isobel: 'Fielding Gray has written to say that Masie Malcolm is in a coma and not expected to come out of it. I wonder why Rosie didn't remember to tell me that? She's very fond of Maisie.'

'Rosie does not like people to be ill,' said Oenone. 'She will not talk about them. Once, when I had a snuffle, she was very unkind all day long and told me not to whine about it.'

'Quite right too,' said Isobel. 'All this silly fuss about health these days. What we really need is for everyone over seventy-five to be dead, instead of cluttering the place up and costing a lot of good money.'

'Which, of course,' said Jo-Jo, 'should be suppressed or locked away.'

'Item,' said Isobel, rubbing her bum lubriciously on the lid of the sarcophagus, 'Jeremy has written.'

'Oenone likes Jeremy,' Oenone said.

'Well, you may see him before long. Apparently he and Fielding and Camilla Salinger and that little Italian quean, Caspar, are coming out to stay at the swish hotel down the road at Barbazon. Come to think of it, there was a hint about that in Fielding's letter. Jeremy is writing a few days later and he's quite positive.'

'Oh dear,' said Jo-Jo. 'What a lot of money is going to be let loose in that clippy hotel. Does Jeremy say *why* they're coming? It can hardly be for a holiday at this time of the year.'

'It seems that they've caught the Cathar bug, like Jean-Marie,' Isobel said. 'They are particularly interested in later Cathar doctrine and ritual, i.e. what the Cathars got up to in the later thirteenth century, well after Simon de Montfort's anti-Cathar Crusade, and even in the fourteenth.'

'They'll be a little too far west just here,' said Jo.

'I don't know. Jean-Marie seems quite happy working here.'

'Jean-Marie is still reading the subject up . . . when not making experiments in vegetarian diet, which can be done anywhere.'

'You think the Carmilla contingent will be more aggressive?' said Isobel. 'I dare say you're right. In that case they'll find Foix a very easy run. Also Pamiers and Ax. And they can always move on later. Meanwhile,' she continued, having given her bum a final scrape on the end of the lid, 'one asks oneself how pleased one will be to see them.'

'Oenone will be very pleased to see Jeremy,' Oenone said. 'Oenone wants to sit in Jeremy's lap, like she did when she was a baby.'

'Oenone,' said Isobel, 'is growing much too big to sit in people's laps.'

'What rubbish,' said Jo-Jo; 'I often sit on yours.'

She did so now. Oenone came and sat on hers.

'Like that picture of the Virgin on her mother's lap,' said Isobel, 'and Christ on the Virgin's.'

'Oenone hasn't got a little banana between her legs,' said Oenone, 'like Christ has in all the pictures.'

'You're very well without it,' said Isobel.

'I always wished I had a banana,' said Jo-Jo; 'so convenient for pissing . . . I think, Isobel, that we shall be *quite* pleased to see them when they arrive. It will at least make a change. We must give them all dinner. Living as we do in a church, we have not the amenities to entertain at home. We shall have to take them out. There is an hotel with an excellent restaurant at St-Girons.'

'Too far away.'

'Too expensive is what you mean. Very well, Isobel, you manky old tight-twot. If you are too mingy to buy your old friends dinner, then I shall pay.'

'It's not just a matter of meanness – '

'No?'

'I honestly think that to throw so much money about is vulgar and offensive,' Isobel said.

'Do you want to come or not?'

'Yes. I want to see Fielding again.'

'Oenone wants to come. She wants to see Jeremy again. Oenone has no money,' said Oenone, 'so she can't pay anything.'

'That's all right, precious,' said Jo-Jo. 'Mummy will pay in order to shame Auntie Isobel.'

'I shan't be in the least shamed, thank you.'

'When are they coming?'

'The day after tomorrow,' Isobel said.

'Goodie,' said Oenone; 'goodie, goodie. But that is the day after tomorrow. Will Auntie Isobel please buy Oenone an ice-lolly now?'

118

'Why does she always ask me and not you?' said Isobel. 'You're her mother.'

'And you're the one that loves her.'

'You called her "precious" just now.'

'A mere *façon de parler*,' said Jo-Jo. 'I do like sitting on your lap.'

'You just said I was a manky old tight-twot.'

'Another *façon de parler*. I, of all people, know how hot and juicy you really are.'

'Time to get off,' said Isobel; 'this is Holy Ground, when all is said. Let us go and buy your daughter an ice-lolly. We're going now,' she called through the tracery (rather spare for Gothic) to Jean-Marie down in the meadow.

Jean-Marie raised a hand in farewell, but did not look up or cease gathering grass.

Raisley Conyngham invited Marius Stern to tea in his chambers, in order to check up on one thing and another.

'Are you sure,' Raisley began, 'that you have done your work properly for O levels?'

'Of course, sir.'

'You were away for a lot of last Quarter. We can't afford to have you mess up this exam through carelessness or complacency.'

'I know, sir. I took several books with me to Italy when I went with Caspar, and did quite a lot of hard reading, particularly when we were hanging about in Terracina.'

'Good. Next question: have you heard from Lady Canteloupe whether Canteloupe still wants a son? And if so, whether you are the chosen father?'

'Is this an inquisition, sir?'

'Don't be insolent, boy. Answer me.'

Marius went pale.

'There will be no more of that, sir. Theodosia and I are

119

not on the best of terms. She has now written to say that Canteloupe is much taken by the little Lady Nausikaa and has decided, to her great relief, not to press her to become pregnant again.'

'What else did she say?'

It was on the tip of Marius' tongue to tell his pedagogue to mind his own business, when Raisley smiled and passed a plate of egg sandwiches.

'Made with Heinz Salad Cream,' Raisley said. 'An odd taste, some would say, but it is your taste.'

'And you have remembered it,' said Marius, absurdly touched. His green eyes flashed at Raisley Conyngham as he piled a very greedy allowance of sandwiches on to his plate. 'Lady Canteloupe rebuked me in her letter, sir, for not attending Jenny's funeral. She said that I had received kindness from Jenny. I had told her, you see, what passed between me and Jenny last spring. Kindness indeed. Yet I still felt no obligation to go to the funeral.'

'Quite right. There is never any obligation,' said Raisley Conyngham, 'to attend a funeral. Why should you or anybody else be obliged to follow a box full of decomposing animal matter and watch as it is put into a hole?'

'But in this case? I had received, as Thea urged and as I admit . . . and as you, sir, very well know . . . great kindness from Jenny.'

'All that is over,' said Raisley Conyngham, 'was over before ever she was dead.'

'Kindness received can never be over, sir.'

'Then remember it, if you must. Say a prayer for the poor ghost that wanders by Cocytus, if you will. But do not inconvenience yourself on this account. That funeral would have meant at least a day spent away from your work. There are no duties towards a corpse except to ensure its burial, and if others take care of that, as they did in this case, then there are, *tout simple*, no duties towards a corpse.'

'But towards a memory, sir?'

'I have already told you,' said Conyngham with slight irritation, 'that you may remember and pray as you please, provided none of this distracts you too long from more important matters. Now then; there is a story that Major Fielding Gray, and his friend and yours, Jeremy Morrison, may be going, with others, on an expedition of historical research. What do you know of any such expedition?'

'Carmilla Salinger told me during Valentine's Exit that she was going with them. I asked her to let me come, but she wouldn't.'

'A very good thing she won't. You had enough time off before Christmas.'

'She nearly did. She was angry about some things – that disagreement I had with her about Jeremy and his journey last autumn – but now that's all over I think she still likes me a lot. Yet in the end she was firm that I could not go with her and the rest. I think Piero Caspar is of the party. I should have liked the chance to talk more with him.'

'Talking with Piero Caspar is dangerous work but excellent training. More of this later. Meanwhile, what is this historical research? Did Carmilla say?'

Conyngham, of course, knew very well what was this historical research. But he wanted to hear Marius tell him, as a proof of the boy's loyalty and as a final confirmation of the facts.

'It's all to do with something called the Albigensian or Cathar heresy, sir . . . something derived from the Manichaeans, I think. They are to start looking . . . for whatever they are looking for . . . near a place called St-Bertrand-de-Comminges, where they have found rather a decent hotel with two rosettes for its food in the *Guide*

Michelin. Later, they may go on to Narbonne and Beziers.'

No doubt then, thought Raisley, as he passed Marius the plate of egg sandwiches: time to be off, he thought. I shall need leave of absence; I shall simply say that there are sudden and urgent reasons for checking the research for which I was given a sabbatical in 1975 and '76. I shall also need help when I get there. It would have been amusing to take Marius and use him against his friends, but since he must stay here (I entirely agree with Carmilla) and make sure of a sound result in his wretched but essential examination, I shall invite Milo Hedley. He only has his Prelims this summer – no great matter – and I can make everything all right through that flabby fellow, Dean ffoliott-Hume. Yes: Milo, decorative, devious and dedicated Milo, will be just the companion for a frolic in Cathar country.

PART THREE
The Nesting Place

Quivi le brutte Arpie lor nidi fanno,
  che cacciar de le Strofade i Troiani
  con tristo annunzio di futuro danno.

(Hither, to roost, the loathsome Harpies fly,
  who chased the Trojans from the Strophades
  with dismal presage of mischief drawing nigh.)

Dante: *Inferno*, Canto 13, lines 10 to 12
Trans: Geoffrey L. Bickersteth

As soon as his mind was made up about his forthcoming expedition to the Languedoc, Raisley Conyngham summoned Milo Hedley from Cambridge; and the following weekend Milo Hedley came.

'I am taking you for a cure at Lourdes,' said Raisley to Milo, as they walked by the river in the valley beneath the school.

'I applaud your generosity, sir, but would wish it diverted to a more agreeable locality. Lourdes,' said Milo, 'is a pilgrim town; it is infested with the sour uses of piety and wholly without *une bonne table*. Why – for Christ's sake, sir – why Lourdes?'

'I told you. For a cure. Spiritual rather than physical, Milo. I do not propose to have you submerged in a miraculous pool, but to open your bigoted mind to the possibilities of psychic visions – of many varieties.'

'Again, sir: why Lourdes?'

'It is well situated for our purpose. No one will look for us there. Our opponents have taken as their headquarters a luxurious and therefore prominent hotel a little way to the east: we shall practise tactful and tactical humility, Milo, in a pilgrims' hotel.'

'I think, sir, that I should sooner be luxurious and prominent.'

'This is not a holiday, Milo.'

'I suppose not. Who are these "opponents"?'

'Marius' so-called friends who wish him to be rid of you and me.' Raisley Conyngham listed the members of Carmilla's team. 'They have discovered that since my

125

boyhood I have been interested in the Cathars, and that I have made long and quite frequent excursions to their country, on the edge of which lies a charming little town called St-Bertrand-de-Comminges . . . and near it the commodious hotel of which I speak. They will issue out of this daily, seeking to hit upon the paths which I once trod and so to discover matter to my grave discredit.'

'Why should your excursions in this area have left evidence of discredit?' Milo Hedley smiled his mysterious and carefully practised smile in imitation of an Archaic statue of a Greek kouros.

'I know you think that smile suits you, Milo,' Raisley Conyngham said, 'but what sits well on a face of pure marble does not sit so well on the pasty and pustular features of a run-down undergraduate. You have been neglecting your health, not taking fresh air and exercise. I shouldn't wonder if you have been doping. You need the care and influence of a civilized and moderate man. I shall attend to your diet and your physical regimen as well as your spiritual education.'

'You haven't answered my question, sir: what evidence of discredit could you possibly have left on your earlier progressions through this region?'

'Many of the Cathars, Milo, particularly the later ones, believed that the Devil was not only the enemy of God, but an *equal enemy*, and was as powerful in the dissemination of Evil (in which we may include certain kinds of Pleasure) as God was in the promotion of Good.'

'So I have heard.'

'Then consider the case of those that worshipped the Devil, on the ground that he was the equal of God and might even, in the end, conquer God. You may imagine that their ceremonies were, to say the least, picturesque, Milo.'

'But in no way discreditable to you, who were only investigating them.'

'A proper investigation often necessitates a re-creation, a re-enactment. And if one finds people sympathetic to such enterprises, Milo, the re-enactment may be crowded and vigorous.'

'I see, sir. You've thrown a few merry and mucky black masses and left the remains of a sacrifice or two lying about. Now you're afraid that the opposition may discover these remains, and you want me to help you head them off. But rather than say so directly, sir, you take refuge in all this clap-trap about my spiritual or psychical enlightenment.'

'I find you disappointingly crude, Milo. I always thought Trinity was an unsatisfactory college, despite the presence there of my friend, Dean ffoliott-Hume. What has become of you in the last six months? However, I shall try once more. You will have heard that the Cathars or Albigensians believed in a Demiurge, who created the natural universe in order to spite God. Later Cathars, as I have been explaining, believed that this Demiurge, or Devil, was equal in power or capacity to God. This belief survived into the fourteenth and even into the fifteenth century. Quite a lot of people still know of it and find it – well, amusing.'

'And these helped you to get your witches' covens together?'

'Milo, Milo. Witchcraft depended on a Devil who was known and acknowledged by his followers to be inferior to God and ultimately doomed. Those that practised Witchcraft were the desperate victims of a death-and-damnation wish. But this faith which I am talking of was a faith in a mighty Demiurge who was the equal and co-eternal enemy of God, a faith in a Devil who had existed on a par with God from the Beginning of Beginnings,

127

Amen. Those that subscribed to such a faith hoped to live and rule for ever. They did not assemble in *covens*. Nor do their descendants assemble in such a squalid fashion now.'

'Their descendants do not assemble at all – or didn't,' said Milo, 'until you got it all going again. Or so you seem to imply.'

'Let's say that I was able to formulate and then create for others some impression of what the worship of the Cathar Satan, the alternative God, entailed. This was a tremendous, an awesome thing, Milo; not just a gaggle of a few old men and women masturbating over pubescent flesh.'

'Whichever way you look at it, sir, *something* might have been left behind which you don't want the opposition to discover.'

'On the contrary, Milo. I want to guide them to it, involve them in it. For whatever is left behind is not just petty and messy, it is deep and serious and numinous matter. By making them privy to it, I shall hoist them with their own petard.'

Milo skimmed a flat stone across the river and rocketing into the bushes the other side.

'There spake the Master,' he grinned. 'Now as ever, sir, I stay or go as your man. But just tell me this: how am I to get leave of absence from Trinity in the middle of term?'

'Just go to Dean ffoliott-Hume and say, "My master hath need of me: prithee, sir, let me go." A little joke we used to have together in the old days – not that I was ever very closely associated with him. But you will find your reference to our little pleasantry will be quite enough to persuade him to release you until the end of term.'

* * *

In the end, it was decided that Oenone was too young, by English standards if not by French, to join Jo-Jo's party for Carmilla & Co. in St-Girons. Oenone was easily reconciled to the disappointment when Jeremy volunteered to stay with her in the deconsecrated chancel in which she lived with her parents and Isobel Stern.

As soon as she was alone with Jeremy, Oenone dropped her childish habit of referring to herself in the third person.

'I have been longing and longing to meet you again,' Oenone said to Jeremy as they sat over the fire in the chimney into which Jo-Jo's money (and a little, much grudged, of Isobel's) had converted the turret over the North East Oratory. 'I have been longing to meet you again, Jeremy, ever since you carried me in the back of Isobel's car, that time we went to Venice.'

'But you were only a few weeks old, Oenone. You can't possibly remember what happened.'*

'I remember because I have often been reminded, Jeremy. Mummy will say to Isobel, "Do you remember how kind Jeremy was to Oenone, that time we drove to Venice, how Jeremy held her in the back, while I watched your legs quiver over the great Lagonda gears in the front." And then I shall feel as if I am lying in your arms, while the huge Lagonda carries us across Italy to Venice. Let me lie in your arms now, Jeremy.'

'You are a big girl now, Oenone, not a baby.'

'Not too big to lie in your arms, Jeremy. On your lap. If you let me come on to your lap, I shall tell you things about our life in France. I always listen, you see, to what the grown-ups say. And to what others say . . . to the ghosts round this chancel.'

* See *The Face of the Waters* by S. R. (Muller, Blond & White, 1985 or GraftonBooks)

'Ghosts?'

'Let me lie in your arms and I will tell you.'

'Very well.'

After a while, Oenone said:

'You have seen the grave-ground round the chancel?'

'Yes.'

'Part of it is very old. There are lots of stone coffins, as there are in the cloister up at the Cathedral. I love that cloister, Jeremy.'

She nuzzled at his breast, as if he had been her wetnurse, so that her voice was muffled and he heard her with some difficulty.

'My father, Jean-Marie, is always hunting about among the tombs and the coffins, both here and in the cloister. He talks to me as he searches, but sometimes his voice frightens me because it is not only his but many more, the voices of the ghosts of the people who once lay in the coffins. Sometimes I am so frightened that I will not go with him for many days, but always I go again in the end.'

'What do the voices say?' murmured Jeremy into her soft hair.

'My father says, "This is a black coffin, a black tomb." He knows because it is marked with a tiny black figure, a tiny little pin-man, inside, on the left hand of the space in which the head once lay.'

'What is the pin-man doing, Oenone?'

'He is kneeling and worshipping with his arms wide and his knees spread. "One of Satan's own," my father will say. "A black figure makes a black tomb." Then other voices come. "We have left our hair and our nails," the voices say, "that the *domus* may continue." What is a "*domus*", Jeremy?'

'A *domus* is a house, a home, a family. Surely your father told you that?'

'It is no longer Jean-Marie's voice. I trust the wine is to your liking?'

'Oh yes. Are you comfortable?' Jeremy said.

'Just let me lie here like this. "They take our hair and our nails and sometimes our manly parts from our groins," the voices say, "that these may remain in the *domus* and make it fertile and prosperous. The rest of our bodies they place in black tombs. The tombs with the black figures are for those that go with the Satan-God, who made the Universe and all the beauty and pleasure within it. Ours is a black *domus*. Others, who die in a white *domus*, die, as we do, without the blessing of the Church and its priests, but these are placed in white tombs and do not lose their nails and their hair and their manhood. These are those who believe themselves perfect, who eat only grass and have renounced the Satan-God and go with the white God of Heaven who knows nothing of the earth. These say, as once, long ago, all of our people said, that the white God is the pure and holy God, the mightier God; but for many years now more and more of our people have gone with the Satan-God. For the Satan-God is the God of joy: he makes our mothers and our sisters and our daughters to worship us according to the rite."'

'You imagine all this, Oenone. It is your father's voice, partly talking to you, partly muttering and speculating to himself.'

'I might be your daughter, Jeremy. Let me worship you according to the rite.'

'Has your father told you of this rite?'

'No: other voices. They say that you should worship any person whom you love. No matter whom. All is permitted. I myself have worshipped Marius' sister Rosie, whom I love more dearly than any person except you.'

'How . . . how have you worshipped her?'

'I have stroked and kissed her beautiful, long black

131

hair. To worship a person, Jeremy, you choose whatever you love most in them, whatever is most beautiful, to caress and kiss. In you I should choose your smooth, round, white neck. This worship is the joy of those who go into the black coffins. The pure and perfect, who go into the white coffins, have no such joy.'

There was a step in the aisle of the chancel. Oenone rose, without haste, from Jeremy's embrace and went to the entrance of the oratory.

'Poppa,' she called. 'Oenone and Jeremy have been talking of you . . . of your search among the coffins and the tombs.'

Jean-Marie Guiscard lifted his daughter and carried her into the oratory. He looks twice his age, Jeremy thought: his face is wizened: much study is weariness of the flesh.

'They were all boring at that dinner,' Jean-Marie said to Oenone and Jeremy. 'Your friend, Carmilla Salinger, does not understand what she is looking for. Nor does the man with one eye and the military title – Major Fielding Gray. The little Italian may understand, but he is now English of the English, and will understand less and less. As for my wife and Isobel Stern, all they do is bicker about politics and money – and about Oenone's education.'

'Oenone wants to stay here,' said Oenone, 'with Jean-Marie, her kind Poppa, and Isobel and Jeremy.'

'Jeremy will not be here very long,' he said.

Oenone gave him a poker-faced look and said nothing.

'So you simply came straight home,' said Jeremy, lifting his eyes from Oenone's face to Jean-Marie's just above it.

'By taxi. No one else took the slightest notice. They ignored me.'

'They pretended to ignore you,' Jeremy said. 'But Fielding was very conscious of you as a rival writer. Piero Caspar, now that he has become, as you say, "English of

132

the English", was practising how to despise a foreigner in the English manner. Carmilla, the scholar, is worried lest you are more learned than she is. Isobel and your wife of course excluded you.'

'All rather unkind.'

'You will not find me unkind. Nor Oenone. She will worship you after the black Cathar rite, if you wish. Your ruminations have taught her how.'

'I have said too much in front of her.'

'I do not hear only you, Poppa. There are the other voices.'

'The Cathar rites seem harmless enough,' said Jeremy, 'according to what Oenone has just been telling me.'

'Black Cathar rites. The idea is to tempt. A harmless physical contact at first mounts, very slowly, to suggestion, then, even more slowly, to temptation, then to desire, then to hot lust, then to raging comos.'

'With Oenone it would remain innocent. She has worshipped, for example, Rosie Stern's beautiful long black hair.'

'Even with Oenone it will not remain innocent for long,' said Jean-Marie. 'Temptation comes earlier than you think to those who worship.' He set Oenone down and staggered slightly, as if the effort of carrying her had exhausted him, then passed both his hands through his thin hair. Dandruff floated down like snow. 'You must not listen,' he said to his daughter; 'not to my voice nor to any voice.'

'It is impossible, Poppa, for Oenone not to listen.'

'Oenone has been talking of black tombs or coffins,' said Jeremy to Jean-Marie: 'does the phrase "Red Gold from Black Tombs" mean anything to you? I heard it not long ago.'

'It could mean the money,' said Jean-Marie, 'that orthodox Catholic informers got for betraying the dead

133

followers of the Satan-God to the Inquisition, so that the Church could curse or violate the graves and trace and arraign the living relatives.'

'Would the White Cathars – the pure and perfect – also betray the tombs of the Black to the Church?'

'Oh no. The Catholic Church hated White Cathars as much as it did the Black – more, perhaps, because of their manifest holiness. There could never be any sort of alliance between them and the Church. You see, though the White Cathars might deplore the Black, they both shared the same basic belief – that the Satan-God had made the physical universe. White Cathars abominated the Satan-God; they thought he was in some sense inferior to the Good God – a fallen angel, perhaps – or that even if he was equal he would in the end lose the struggle between them. So the White Cathars renounced the physical universe and all its pleasures. Black Cathars embraced such pleasures, believing that they were created by a God that was in any case equal and might ultimately prove superior to the Good God.'

'Surely, the White Cathars, the "Perfects", sometimes converted the others on their death bed.'

'Sometimes. Sometimes not. But in no case whatever did the White Cathars think like Priests of the Catholic Church. White Cathars believed in a Dualism – an horrendous heresy to true Catholics – as firmly as did the Black, though the emphasis was different.'

'So those that sought Red Gold from Black Tombs would always be Roman Catholics in good standing, hoping for the rewards of delation?'

'Yes, though this phrase "Red Gold from Black Tombs" could bear a different, a metaphorical interpretation. It could mean the relics that Black Cathars took from the coffins of their fellows. These were normally cut from the corpses when they were in their coffins but

134

before the coffins were closed. So in a sense the relics came from the tomb.'

'Some people also worshipped the dead bodies before the coffins were closed,' Oenone said. 'Or so the voices say. The women worshipped the dead bodies of the men, and the men of the women . . . to make up for taking the relics. The relics, you see, were to make the *domus* strong for the future; they would not have done this unless those from whom they were taken were worshipped and loved before they were buried.'

'No more of this,' said Jean-Marie in a rather desperate voice. 'Your mother was right. We should have sent you back to England to a boarding school.'

'What boarding school?' Oenone enquired. 'Isobel said there is only one proper boarding school left, the one Baby Canteloupe went to many years ago, and that will not accept girls as young as me. Jeremy will put Oenone to bed now, in the organ loft. Oenone liked it very much when Jeremy put her to bed while she was still a baby. It will be even nicer now that I am old enough to appreciate him properly . . . his soft white hands and his kind touch. Poppa must come too; Poppa must not be jealous.'

Oenone preceded Jean-Marie, who preceded Jeremy, up the winding stair and into the organ loft.

'Jo-Jo often tells me how you cared for the infant Oenone in the back of the Lagonda,' said Jean-Marie. 'She and Isobel talk of it so often that Oenone thinks she remembers it.'

'What are these voices?' Jeremy said. 'These voices that speak to her?'

Oenone set about washing herself all over from the basin that had been put in to replace the keyboard of the organ.

'Look at Oenone washing herself,' she said. 'She will need kind hands to dry her.'

'Young children do hear such things,' said Jean-Marie in a false voice to Jeremy. 'They have fantasies.'

He is trying to forget his fear, thought Jeremy: to persuade himself that everything is all right after all, despite what he said just now. He wants her to stay here, as she does. Aloud he said:

'Young children do not normally have fantasies about females that "worship" their sons and brothers and fathers.'

'All part of her tender little infantile Eden,' said Jean-Marie. 'You yourself said it was innocent.'

'And you yourself said it wasn't – or would not long remain so,' said Jeremy. 'Quite apart from anything else, she already talks of what is done to corpses in their coffins.'

'Dry Oenone with kind hands,' Oenone said. She gave a warm towel (heated in the case which once contained the bellows) to Jeremy and another to Jean-Marie. 'That will be lovely. The people who go into the black coffins are the followers of joy.'

'Of love,' said Jeremy; 'or so we may hope.'

'Of temptation,' said Jean-Marie. 'I tell you, *ma chèrie*, that if you are to stay here with us, you must hear no more voices.'

'How can Oenone help hearing voices if they speak to Oenone? Always, Poppa, after you speak, they speak.'

'Then I shall speak to you no more,' her father said.

'You must. Or Oenone will hate you. Help me put my nightie on.'

After a lot of clumsy fumbling with the garment both by Jeremy and Jean-Marie the night-dress descended over Oenone's innocent form. She climbed into the little bed beneath the crucifix of the rood-screen. Without another word she closed her eyes.

* * *

Milo Hedley went to see Dean ffoliott-Hume of Trinity, a man gross yet dandified, with a face like that of an adult and disillusioned cherub.

'"My master hath need of me,"' Milo quoted Raisley Conyngham: '"prithee, sir, let me go."'

Ffoliott-Hume looked shaken, then wobbled all over.

'Has your Master any message for me?' he enquired.

'No, sir. Only the request I have just spoken in my own behalf.'

'He never has need of me now,' whined ffoliott-Hume. 'Not for seventeen years has he had need of me.' He started to cry in rather a feeble way, as though his favourite aunt had died and had not, despite her promises, left him any money. 'Then go to your Master,' he said through his sobs: 'return by mid-April; until then you may serve your Master with my blessing.'

As Milo approached the door, ffoliott-Hume added, snivelling and dribbling, 'You may serve him with your whole heart now, but in the end he will abandon you, if it suits him, just as he has abandoned me. He abandons even the most loyal of his servants.'

I wonder whether he will abandon Marius, thought Milo, hope rising.

'Thank you, Dean,' he said to ffoliott-Hume: 'thank you for the tip.'

'Jean-Marie Guiscard,' said Jeremy to Carmilla, as they walked in the winter woods round Barbazon the morning after Jo-Jo's dinner at St-Girons and Jeremy's conversation with Oenone and her father, 'Jean-Marie Guiscard has written several passable books.'

'He rates pretty fair as an amateur scholar,' said Carmilla with condescension.

'His best was probably the one about the Castle at

Arques,'* said Jeremy: 'He has – or had – a deft way of dealing with the occult, of making it appear more or less natural, at worst a nuisance or an inconvenience rather than something horrible or perverse.'

'And so?' Carmilla said.

'He is now studying the Cathars. But this time he is not treating the occult lightly and deftly, he is making heavy weather, black heavy weather. I know this because Oenone . . . whom I have known well from the time she was a baby . . . took me into her confidence and told of some of the things which Jean-Marie has been saying. She also claims that there are "other voices", which begin when Jean-Marie ceases and say even more macabre things than he does. But I think she imagines this – or perhaps wishes to attribute the foul things that are said to someone other than her father, of whom she is obviously fond.'

'What . . . foul things?'

'Suggestions of incest and ritual manipulation of corpses in their coffins; the dismantling of cadavers to provide magic objects, and to preserve the strength and prosperity of the dead to assist the *domus* or household to a prosperous future. This is what Jean-Marie and "the voices" have been talking of to Oenone. As I say, I think "the voices" are merely the voice of Jean-Marie which probably becomes more excited or agitated as his discourse continues, giving Oenone an excuse to predicate a spokesman other than her father.'

'Does Oenone understand these things?' Carmilla asked.

'She has heard a lot of things, which little girls do not usually hear, from her mother and her mother's lover,

---

* *September Castle* and *Morning Star* by S. R. (Muller, Blond & White, 1983, Muller, Blond & White, 1984 or GraftonBooks)

Isobel Stern. She is evidently conscious that even very little girls can exercise some kind of physical enticement; when going to bed last night she showed herself off to me and her father.'

'Which,' said Carmilla, 'is all very ill for Oenone and not much help to us. I thought it was a mistake to come here so soon, without further consideration.'

'The only mistake would be to despond so soon. You remember what Glastonbury had to say on that Christmas card which was intended for Raisley Conyngham but was sent by mistake to our old "Chamberlain" at Luffham?'

'Something about Red Gold and Black Tombs?'

'Right. Jean-Marie speaks of "Black Tombs" or "Coffins", with small black images on the inside, near where the head would rest. He thinks these coffins were those of "Black" Cathars, i.e. those that had chosen to follow and adore the "Satan-God", as opposed to "White" Cathars who obeyed the "Good God" of Heavenly Light. He had theories about what "Red Gold" could mean in this context . . .'

'The trouble with all this stuff of Jean-Marie's,' said Piero Caspar over luncheon in the hotel at Barbazon, 'is this: he posits a Devil who is not only *de facto et de jure* the equal of God but one who may also succeed in overcoming him. But any such total victory must surely be highly improbable, given equality and co-eternity (that is, an equality which has already lasted for an eternity) in the subjects in question. The probability, even the certainty, must be that they will remain evenly balanced, neither of them finally victorious over the other nor indeed wishing to be (for has not equality suited them very well for the Eternity past), for all the Eternity to come, i.e. for ever. This means that a human being can choose between them without fear of penalty. This, in turn, makes the rules very different from those which govern, for example, Black Magic. Black Magicians perpetrate their evil in the name of a perpetually *subordinate* Devil, probably a disgraced archangel or seraph. The satisfaction that the practitioners of Black Magic obtain lies in slaking their hatred of the Good and Beautiful and Supreme God by occasionally bringing off annoying forays into his domain. Such practitioners are doomed and know themselves to be so. There is therefore something heroic (no matter how perverse) in their endeavours.

'Now Catharism, on the other hand, has always made things easy for its adherents. Even in its early days, when the Good God of Light was considered by Cathars to be incontestably superior and the Devil or Satan merely a noisome creature of material temptation – even *then* you were still allowed, by the tenets of the Cathar belief, to spend your life among diabolical and fleshly pleasures but at the last to repent, with the assistance of a so-called "perfect, parfait or perfectus", on your death bed, after which you would go unscathed to your reward with the God of Spiritual Light in Heaven. Among later Cathars things were made even easier. No need, now, of death-bed repentance, with the lifelong risk of falling suddenly under a bus, so to speak, and having no opportunity to repent. Repentance was quite beside the point. All you had to do was choose whether to support the Satanic God or the Spiritual God, and whichever you chose would take care of you for ever.'

'You are forgetting one thing,' said Fielding Gray. 'From first to last *all* Cathars were hunted down and burned at the stake by the Inquisition and the agents of orthodox Catholicism. This at least Cathars had in common with Black Magicians and Witches. And again, however different the theory, the Satanic Cathars did, in

140

effect, adopt practices and customs very similar to those of classical Witchcraft.'

'Enough of your theories,' said Carmilla. 'Where does all this lead us?'

'It must lead us,' said Jeremy, 'to the Black Tombs and Coffins, those marked with the little black figure who is kneeling (to judge from Oenone's description) both in adoration and with thighs splayed in lust. Now, in the graveyards of this part of France there is often, though not always, an area of early graves and of loose and scattered sarcophagi, exhumed or exposed for various reasons but in any case now vulnerable to interference and inspection. There are not so many here in Barbazon and St-Bertrand-de-Comminges because, as Jesty Hyphen told Carmilla and Piero, this is very much the border of Cathar country, not the heartland. I suggest investigation of tombs and coffins, here and elsewhere. I also suggest that if we can locate a typical *domus* or family house of the thirteenth or fourteenth century, we have a very close look at that.'

'Shall we go to Foix?' said Fielding. 'Or Ax-les-Thermes? Or Pamiers?'

'I have been reading an interesting book,' said Piero, 'by a Frenchman (*not* Jean-Marie Guiscard) and called *Montaillou*. It deals with the period that most concerns us – the early to mid-fourteenth century, by which time the doctrine of an equal dualism between Satan-God and Good-God was well established. I have here a note of a passage which intrigued me . . . a quotation from a Cathar preacher who was addressing the shepherds of Montaillou, *not*, of course, in the church: "Satan entered into the Kingdom of the Father," said this preacher, "and told the Spirits of that Kingdom that he, the Devil, owned a much better Paradise. 'Spirits, I will bring you into my world,' said Satan, 'and I shall give you oxen, cows, riches and a wife for company . . .'" You see?' said Piero, neatly dissecting a pigeon. 'Easy access from the Earthly Paradise to the Spiritual one. No hostility on either side. Satan, boastful but not overweening, clearly planning nothing much against God except to win over a few of his adherents, fearing nothing from him though on his territory . . . If these were the kind of views that obtained in Montaillou in 1300 or thereabouts, it might be a suitable place for us to begin our research.'

'Does Montaillou still exist?' asked Fielding Gray.

'A ruin in the mountains near Prades,' Piero said, 'not far from an attractive watering-place called Molitq-les-Bains. If we could find a Cathar *domus* there . . . or a Black Coffin buried on or near the premises . . .'

'What could they tell us?' said Carmilla.

'They could tell us whatever they told Raisley Conyngham,' said Jeremy, 'during his various expeditions among these ruins or those like them. They could point us in whatever direction, and towards whatever enormity, they pointed him.'

'How very agreeable,' said Fielding Gray. 'A picnic in the hills tomorrow, near Montaillou. It will make a change from this pretentious dining room. But a teeny bit chilly at this time of the year?'

'We can eat in the car,' said Piero. 'The batteries are specially charged for such an emergency!'

'All these towns of pilgrimage,' said Raisley Conyngham to Milo Hedley, 'have the same dreary texture made up of middle-class humbug mixed with puerile credulity. Lisieux, Rocamadour, Assisi. . . . However seemly the town may be (as with Assisi) or unseemly (as with Lisieux), there is the same underlying and unpalatable moral gristle – the same stupidity and ignorance, the same mistrust of secular knowledge and worldly grace. I verily believe, however, that Lourdes is the most distasteful of all such places. The whole spirit of Lourdes is symbolized by the mass-produced plastic madonna – '

' – Or the souvenir statuette of some witless peasant girl rendered visionary,' said Milo, 'by non-stop masturbation while watching her sheep.'

'Do not elaborate overmuch, Milo. Now then. Our prey. The hunters who will themselves be hunted. They are interested in Raisley Conyngham the Albigensian, the dabbler in Catharism. They think, you see, that he dabbled until his fingers reached filth which he then stirred vigorously in order to see what hideous creatures would emerge from it. Perhaps they are not so wrong (in their own terms) as all that.'

They came to a roundabout. Raisley selected the road to Pau. They drove out of the dismal suburbs of Lourdes, passing some cowed foothills of the Pyrenees which were over to their left.

'Pau?' said Milo. 'We are going away from what is called the action. They will be directing their attention to known Cathar districts – Tarascon or Junac or Sarbathès.'

'Indeed they will, Milo. And in all of those places I have agents or correspondents who will make sure that there is a satisfactory (though never spectacular) show for them. Tasteless vulgarity must be avoided: just enough material provided to tempt the seekers on to the next stage. My correspondents know all about that. They have been sought out, sought out and tested over many years, Milo, during long periods in 1955 and 1956 or in 1975 and '76, during shorter periods, visits of two or three days or even just a few hours, of which Carmilla and the rest know nothing. All my agents know and love their subject; they will appreciate exactly how much to exhibit to that overgrown hoyden, Carmilla Salinger, and her pack of chums . . . who for all the world resemble a gang of children in a tale by Enid Blyton.'

'Who are these correspondents, these agents?' Milo said.

'The keepers of the Cathar faith. It is not to be supposed that a movement once so powerful and numerous is now entirely defunct. They are the men and women who saw me searching when I first came here with good old Jesty Hyphen, and they have helped me to search ever since. Wherever Carmilla & Co. may take themselves, Milo, to Ax-les-Thermes or Prades or Carcassone, or even into Andorra, they will find courteous guides to help them to what they wish to see – just enough of it, Milo, not faked but tailored to suit their taste. Meanwhile, you and I can have a pleasant walk on the Promenade at Pau, admiring the distant peaks and watching the local stalwarts play Pelota on the court below the terrace; and later on we might take tea in the Casino and, greatly daring, try a little roulette.'

'The most important part of a *domus*, or *ostal* as it was called in the vernacular,' said Piero, 'was the inner kitchen where they kept the fire – the sacred fire which must on no account be extinguished. There were rooms adjacent where they slept, two or three to a room, to a bed if necessary. When somebody died, his body would be placed in an open coffin beside the sacred fire in the kitchen.'

The walls which divided the kitchen from the outer rooms and these in turn from the open air were now six inches high. A lugubrious guide held an umbrella over Carmilla as wisps of snow quivered round her amply trousered form.

'The fire would have been about here,' said the guide, pointing to the centre of the 'kitchen'. 'There was no hearth, no chimney – or not here in Montaillou. Perhaps in richer or more elegant towns – '

'And so the coffin would have been laid just here,' said Piero, 'to the east of the fire.'

'With the head by the fire?' suggested Fielding Gray, 'so that if the corpse raised its head it could, theoretically, look towards Jerusalem?'

'A black Cathar would surely wish to look away from Jerusalem,' said Jeremy Morrison.

'I do not know whether such niceties were considered,' Piero said. 'I can simply tell you that the coffin was normally laid to the east of the fire, and that in the case of a black Cathar the coffin would be marked inside, near the head, with a little black figure, as Oenone explained to Jeremy the other night. Hair, nails, possibly one testicle or even both – sometimes the entire ensemble of privata – would be cut away from the corpse to be preserved and ensure the future prosperity and good fortune of the *domus* or *ostal*.'

'That might also be done,' articulated the guide primly, 'even with a white Cathar who worshipped the Good God, though in the latter case probably only hair and nails would be taken, not the genitalia.'

'The coffin would then be sealed,' said Piero, 'and taken out for burial. Possibly the coffin would be placed inside a larger sarcophagus. There were many lying around even then – Roman, you see. Or the body would be taken from the coffin and placed in a sarcophagus, and the sarcophagus marked inside with the little black pin-man (like a primitive cave drawing) adoring and concupiscent. Possibly the sarcophagus would be entombed, if the family was rich, in a vault; or the coffin would be concealed somewhere, if no sarcophagus, Roman or other, was handy. In case of extreme poverty, the body

145

might be buried without the coffin and the coffin kept for future use.'

'How do you come to know so much?' said Fielding Gray. 'I've been reading that book of yours – *Montaillou* – and there's nothing like this in it.'

'I am extrapolating from the customs of my own country,' Piero said.

'You must not use the word "extrapolate",' Carmilla told him. 'It is vulgar jargon, used by louts from the Midlands universities.'

'Forgive a poor bloody foreigner,' Piero smiled thinly then said to the guide, 'Do we know where the burial ground was?'

'By the church, signore,' said the guide, who had spotted that Piero Caspar was Sicilian long before he had apologized for being a foreigner. 'It is, in the words of the English poet, Tennyson, "A broken chancel with a broken cross"; but just as in Tennyson's poem, around it "There lie the mighty bones of ancient men". Or at least, if their bones weren't mighty (for we are taught that ancient men were often of puny build) their tombs were. There is one huge Roman sarcophagus of the kind of which you spoke, inside which are the remains of a coffin of wood, inside which (in turn) is a small tablet. There are no bones or human remains of any kind, but you may find the tablet of great interest. In this case, for whatever reason, the little black pin-man of which you speak was traced, not on the side of the coffin or the sarcophagus, but on the tablet.'

They trudged through whirling snow and stony soil. The church (or rather chapel) was roofless, the west door surmounted by a crude Romanesque tympanum. Not far from this door lay a sarcophagus of which one side and both ends were blank, but the remaining side was carved, in low relief, with a file of ghosts (distinguished as such

146

by grave-clothes) who were led by Hermes with his wand as they cavorted gaily towards a satyr seated on a tree trunk. The satyr was affectionately teaching an eager and unclothed ephebe to play the lyre, while at the same time looking up civilly to greet the arrival of Hermes and the mob in his charge.

The lid of the sarcophagus was leaning against the outer wall of the chapel. The guide leant over one side of the sarcophagus and fished about among some strips and slivers of rotten wood. Eventually he produced a small tablet of rough marble.

'"*Hubertus Nivalis Narbonnensis*",' the guide read from the tablet: '"*Deliciarum Campos petens*." That is, "Hubert Nivale of Narbonne, who seeks the fields of Pleasure." That, madame, messieurs et signore, we may assume to be the Satanic Paradise.'

'How did a man from Narbonne come to die here?' said Fielding.

'How does anyone come to die anywhere?' said Carmilla briskly.

'Narbonne was a long way from here in those days,' Fielding persisted.

'Not too far,' said Carmilla, 'to prevent his making a visit here if there was some matter of importance to be sorted out. But far enough to make it very inconvenient to transport the body back to Narbonne for burial. We may assume that his friends here in Montaillou knew that he was a dualist and a heretic – they were almost certainly so themselves – and therefore had him buried in the appropriate manner. But not, perhaps, without some embarrassment. There was always a risk of spies from the priesthood or the Inquisition. All in all, then, such a man was best buried at once and wherever he died, before word could spread. Least said soonest mended.'

'No names, no pack drill. Then why such a sumptuous

sarcophagus?' said Fielding. 'It could only draw attention.'

'The coffin might have been buried hugger-mugger,' said the guide, 'to borrow a phrase from your national poet, in the best interests of secrecy and celerity. Later, perhaps, time and rough weather exposed and dismantled it; and then a sympathizer, a brother in heresy, who had record in his family of the original swift and sordid interment, might have placed the remains of the coffin in this noble pagan sarcophagus. This work of corporal charity could have been performed centuries after the death of Hubert Nivale, at a period when the Cathar beliefs were no longer punishable or even noticeable.'

'Would records of his original burial have lasted so long?' objected Jeremy.

'Oh yes,' said the guide, bland-faced. 'Records were certainly kept . . . in some cases. As it happens, quite a lot, apart from the circumstances of his burial, is known about Hubert Nivale of Narbonne.'

'What is known?'

'You must go to Narbonne to find that out. The curator of the Museum of Antique Sculpture might assist you. The museum is housed in the huge and deconsecrated Priory Church. Anyone will direct you there.'

'*Hubertus Nivalis*,' said Carmilla. 'Hubert Snowy. Snowy Hubert. A black Cathar, who came from Narbonne – presumably on some affair of moment – and then died in or near Montaillou. How did he die, one wonders? Or of what? There are many more questions to be asked and answered.'

'Some of which, at least,' said Jeremy, 'may apparently be unravelled by the curator of this museum in Narbonne.'

'To be sure, to be sure,' said Carmilla: 'but let us remember the main reason we are here. Our problem is:

148

can we conceivably see Raisley Conyngham in any of this?'

'*Quatorze; rouge, pair et manque,*' announced the croupier.

'Second time running, sir,' said Milo to Raisley Conyngham: 'well done.'

There was only one table in the *Salon des Jeux*. This was placed in the centre of an oval arena fifty yards long by twenty yards wide, canopied by an enormous cupola. Milo and Raisley were the only players and indeed the only clients. Apart from them, the three croupiers and the *chef du parti* there was nobody in the *Salon*, not even the usual hustler to dish out unwanted pencils and paper and breathe down his victim's neck until presented with a tip.

'I wonder,' Milo had said soon after Raisley and he had arrived, 'that they keep the place going at all.'

'There are more people to play later on,' Raisley had said, smirking gently. 'Gamblers come out of holes and corners, you know, like insects at the setting of the sun. However, we shall have left before it gets dark – I hate driving at night.'

Since then Raisley had been winning, off and on. Milo, for the most part, simply watched. When he wagered, he lost.

'The reason I win sometimes,' said Raisley, 'is because I am indifferent. The reason you lose is that you are avid to win. In a word, you are greedy, although you are pretty well supplied with money for this expedition by me.'

'Agreed, sir.'

'One more bet,' Raisley said now.

Raisley left his winning stake on fourteen and directed one of the croupiers by the wheel to treble it, using some of the counters which he had just won. The croupier scowled while he went about this task because Raisley did not tell him to take the customary three per cent of the winning counters and place them in the slot marked 'Service' for the staff.

'*Merci, M'sieur, pour les employés,*' said the croupier sarcastically.

'I was going to tip him and the rest of them when I finally left the table,' said Raisley to Milo: 'now I shall not.'

Raisley's increased bet was now placed and the wheel was spun.

'*Quatorze,*' said the croupier, through his teeth.

'You see?' said Raisley. 'They would have had a very nice *pourboire* indeed from a win like this.'

'Over five hundred quid.'

'Say "pounds", "sovereigns", "Bradburies" – almost anything you choose,' said Raisley, 'but not "quid". Let us not have proletarian usage.'

'Surely, sir, "quid" was perfectly good Edwardian slang.'

'Only among on-the-make Jews of the most slimy kind.'

Raisley rose. He began to pocket the multi-coloured slabs which were piled before him.

'*Merci M'sieur,*' said Raisley to the *chef du parti*. '*Rien pour les employés parce que celui-ci*' – he pointed to the croupier who had thanked him in derision – '*ne fait pas comme il faut.*'

'Canteloupe's Regiment had a motto,' Raisley said to Milo as they walked towards the cashier's desk (Milo carrying the surplus '*plaques*' that would not fit into Raisley's pockets), '"*Res Unius, Res Omnium*" – "the affair of one is the affair of all" – recommending co-operation, you understand, and, one presumes, a just division of the spoils. This little incident provides an amusing example of that motto when it works in reverse.

150

"The fault of one is the fault of all", as is the consequent deprivation. If only the *chef du parti* had disciplined his wretched subordinate for his rebarbative performance, I might have relented.'

'I think, sir, that discipline and morale are low in this Casino.'

'No particular reason why they should be. As I told you, many more clients come by night . . . seeking Red Gold from the Black Wheel. I wonder how our explorers got on today, Milo. Wherever they went, you know, they will have found . . . hints and suggestions to point them further east. And so it will go until they reach the ground and the situation in which I wish to confront them.'

Teresa Malcolm had a telephone call at school, from the Nursing Home in which Maisie Malcolm lay in a coma, and was told that the coma had turned to black death. So she went to find Marius Stern, who was walking up the steps from the Fives courts with friends with whom he had been playing. When they reached the top of the steps, Teresa beckoned to Marius to come to her, and he, seeing what lay in her eyes, at once did her bidding.

'Auntie Maisie is dead,' said Tessa as they walked by the boundary of the cricket ground (where, in the bitter winter, the unseen ghosts were playing their games long past). 'It was very sudden, they said. No awakening and no pain.'

'Auntie Maisie,' echoed Marius. 'Your mother.'

'My mother.'

Shall I tell her, he thought, that it was my father that got her on the body of the whore that was once Maisie Malcolm? No. I shall do as Mr Conyngham tells me. I shall keep my options open.

'Tessa,' he said. 'You know that it is good that she is dead?'

'Yes. And yet I shall miss her.'

'You cannot miss the thing that was lying on the bed in the Nursing Home. She died easily and swiftly, you say, when the time came, and she suffered little or nothing in the time before. And think, Tessa: her friends, those of her age, are growing old and boring and impotent and inept, like poor Fielding Gray; and her younger friends – you and I, and my sister Rosie, and Jakki and Carolyn Blessington – we are all growing up and away from those, like your Auntie Maisie, your mother, who cared for us when we were young. She is better dead, Tessa. Everyone should be dead before the age of seventy, before the pitcher is broken at the fountain: good riddance both for the dead themselves, and for the living.'

'"Some be so strong that they come to fourscore years – "'

'"Yet is their strength then but labour and sorrow, so soon passeth it away and they are gone."'

'Not always,' Tessa said; 'not nowadays, with the new drugs and the new medical knowledge.'

'The new drugs and the new medical knowledge . . . which enable them to escape dying when they should and rot slowly in special homes, slobbering round television sets,' said Marius, 'until they are ninety, ninety-five, a hundred, parcels of flesh being put to bed at six in the evening and being got up again fifteen hours later to face one day more of atrophy, insanity, imbecility – would you wish that for those you love?'

'Can you not speak more kindly of them, Marius?'

'No. I cannot. See here, Tessa: if geriatric care, as I think it is called, continues, at the present rate, to keep larger and larger numbers of very old people alive (or what the doctors euphemistically call "alive"), in not many years' time the resources, the energy and the wealth of the entire nation will be utterly consumed by the needs

152

of legion upon legion of Tithoni. You know who Tithonus was?'

'The lover of Aurora, who at his request granted him eternal life.'

'Yes. He forgot to ask for eternal youth to go with it. He was unkillable and unspeakable. Do I need to labour the point?'

'I suppose,' said Tessa, who was beginning to hate this conversation and wished at any cost to turn it, 'I suppose,' she said, cheaply but not seeing how else to attain her wish, 'that you resent the idea of all your money being taxed and taken to pay for the comfort of the old?'

Marius laughed.

'They'll tax and take *your* money too,' he said, matching her in cheapness. 'You are going to have rather a lot now, little Tessa. Your auntie, your mummy, will have left you everything.'

'I don't think she had all that much, except her interest in that dismal hotel.'

Marius laughed again.

'Do you realize,' he said, 'what Buttock's Hotel is now worth – simply for its site in the Cromwell Road?'

'The owners are bound in honour not to sell it . . . by the wish and the will of the late Mrs Buttock.'

Marius laughed a third time.

'Honour?' he said. 'Bound in honour by the wish and the will of the late Mrs Buttock? Darling Tessa, these days such a concept can be killed by a deft lawyer in five minutes flat.'

'That woman's dead,' said Isobel Stern to Jo-Jo Guiscard: 'the old Quean of Buttock's Hotel. I've had a letter all about it from Rosie. Here.'

'Dear Mummy,' Rosie wrote and Jo-Jo read, 'I hope Oenone and Jo-Jo and you are all well. I am.'

153

'Do you suppose the first sentence expresses an order of preference?' Isobel interrupted Jo-Jo as she read.

'Very probably,' said Jo-Jo; 'I shall congratulate her on her good taste when I see her.'

'Even although she puts Oenone before you?'

'Her penchant for Oenone is no secret,' said Jo-Jo. 'The fact that I detest the little wretch myself is quite beside the point.'

'And what is that?'

'That she writes what she means, plainly and honestly.' Jo-Jo returned to the letter.

'Auntie Maisie is dead,' wrote Rosie, 'so we all went to the funeral: Teresa, Jakki and Carolyn Blessington, Marius and myself. Jakki and Carolyn's mother and father were going round the world, or some of it, at the time; they are very rich now that Colonel Blessington is employed by our firm.'

'Rosie does not appear to realize,' said Jo-Jo to Isobel, 'that your firm also belongs to the Salingers and the Canteloupes.'

'She knows all that perfectly well,' said Isobel. 'To ignore the others is Rosie's idea of a joke.'

'Here is another,' said Jo-Jo. '"Lord Canteloupe and his friend, Major Glastonbury, also came,"' she read aloud. '"Lord Canteloupe said that since they were both in Major Fielding Gray's old regiment they were representing him, as Major Gray, of all people, should be represented on this occasion."'

'That,' said Isobel, 'is a Canteloupe joke.'

'But here comes the next Rosie one. "Lady Canteloupe didn't come. Perhaps she didn't like the idea of seeing Teresa all in black."'

'I think I can be spared further examples of my daughter's wit,' said Isobel; 'I've read the thing once. She

154

clearly has no social conscience whatever – or is just trying to annoy me.'

'On the whole the funeral was voted a success,' Jo-Jo went back to reading to herself. 'Nothing went positively wrong, and our old chef from Kensington you remember, Ethel and/or Mabel we used to call him – who has been running Buttock's since Mrs Malcolm was taken poorly, put on a magnificent spread back at the hotel: caviar (fresh beluga, Mabel said), golden plovers' eggs (frozen from the season before – totally forbidden and illegal, Ethel told us), and a marvellous dish of baby lobsters and crawfish (also forbidden and illegal). Ethel and/or Mabel has had a lot of names since I last saw him: Christabel, Titania, Clarissa and Lucrezia, to mention only a few; but now he prefers plain Hilda – he says that we live in an era in which it is advisable to be common and will soon be obligatory.

'Anyway, plain Hilda will go on running Buttock's until Fielding gets back, and then, she says, everyone can decide what will be the best thing to do next.

'Odd items of interest. Canteloupe says that his baby daughter is very well, and that he adores her. It seems, however, that Theodosia Canteloupe no longer adores her (if ever she did) and Canteloupe has had to procure a wetnurse from among the peasant women on his estate.

'Marius's friend in Somerset, whom he calls Auntie Flo, has won a small football pool (£2,053 and nine new pence), and got into trouble for making a "racist" remark while celebrating. Apparently she told Thea Canteloupe (with whom she was dining *à deux*) that there is a mysterious new disease, so secret that it hasn't even got a name yet, and that American faggots who go in for buggery (either way) are getting it by the thousands and then dropping dead as soon as they catch so much as a cold in the nose, because this new disease stops you

155

resisting all other illnesses. It was very much worse, said Auntie Flo, in parts of black Africa, where it had probably begun in the first place; but this was meant to be even more secret than what was happening in the US because nowadays we are not allowed to be told anything nasty about blacks. Well, some catering student who was being trained in the restaurant and chanced to be waiting on Thea and Auntie Flo overheard what had been said and immediately made a row, and Auntie Flo was reported to the Race Relations Board. *They* were going to make a show case of it, only Canteloupe's old chum, Doctor La Soeur, produced an expert on African diseases, with every letter in the book after his name, who was prepared to give evidence that A. Flo was telling the truth and nothing but. Even then some of the race fanatics wanted to go on with the case, because they said that A. Flo had spoken in malice and that no one could *prove* this disease had *started* in Africa. But it seemed that Doc. La Soeur's expert, even if he couldn't absolutely prove that, could and would prove so many other things about the blacks and what they'd got that the Race Relations Board had the sense (for once) to shut up.

'So that's all for now. Incidentally, does Major Fielding Gray know that Maisie Malc. is dead? Marius says he's somewhere in your part of France. He didn't send any flowers to Maisie or any message to Tessa. If you see him, let him know – for all the good it will do anybody.

Love to all at St-Bertrand
from Rosie.'

'I suppose,' said Jo-Jo to Isobel, 'that Fielding Gray won't have heard about Maisie – unless he's read about her in the Deaths column of an English paper.'

'There aren't any nearer than Lourdes,' said Isobel;

'and he wouldn't have read them even if there were. I once heard Fielding say that when he was abroad he took it as a God-given dispensation to remain totally ignorant of the imbecilities perpetrated in England.'

'Ought we to tell him?' said Jo-Jo.

'They've gone,' said Isobel: 'the whole group. Carcassone or some such place. Jeremy came especially to say goodbye to Oenone. Just as well that *he's* gone anyhow. He was upsetting both Oenone and Jean-Marie. Now we can resume our accustomed peace and economy.'

'It appears,' said Raisley Conyngham to Milo Hedley over dinner in their hotel (*Les Stigmata Christi*) in Lourdes, 'that old Maisie Malcolm is dead. I have a letter here from Marius which I collected from the *Poste Restante* this evening while you were sleeping in your usual hoggish fashion.'

'It is a French custom to have a nap in the evenings,' said Milo: 'it is called *le cinq à sept*.'

'Yes. A *French* custom,' said Raisley Conyngham. 'You are English, to the best of my belief, and should eschew unwholesome foreign habits. Poor old Maisie: so respectable of late years, so becomingly dressed in her black bombasine. Do you know why retired whores always favour black bombasine, Milo?'

'Penitence, I suppose.'

'Rubbish. Never was a less penitent woman than Maisie. Can they teach you nothing at Trinity? Retired whores favour black bombasine, Milo, because a whore who reaches the stage of retirement (as opposed to a pauper's grave) must be a very prudent, wary and economic woman. She wears black bombasine because she need no longer wear more showy garments, because it lasts a very long time, and because it does not show stains and need be sent infrequently to the laundry. Good old

Maisie. She gave a lot of pleasure in her heyday, Milo. She used to put on lupanal exhibitions of Byzantine ingenuity and Roman enormity. I attended once, and was grossly overcharged.'

'One can hardly expect that sort of a thing to come cheap, sir. Really, I don't know when I last tasted such horrible food.'

'Never forget we are in Lourdes, Milo. We are being punished for our sins.'

'*I* didn't go to Maisie Malcolm's lupanal exhibitions. Why should I be punished?'

'Because you have performed the abominable act with the Honourable Jeremy Morrison.'

'It gave him great pleasure.'

'That is no excuse. It is still a sin. Leave its wickedness aside, I shouldn't, if I were you, dear boy, repeat it. Jeremy has been . . . indiscriminate. Mind you, I'm told that since an odd and uplifting experience he had at Brindisi* late last year, he has elected the way of chastity. But before then he had placed himself well and truly in danger of catching this new carnal infection which comes from California. So don't wander down Memory Lane with Morrison, Milo, even if he lapses from virtue and invites you.'

'This new malady is one of the things we *have* heard about in Trinity, sir. One of the chaps has an uncle who picked it up while on safari in Kenya. It seems that it's spreading so efficiently that with any luck it will halve the population of the world. Just what is needed.'

'Greed and pollution will do the job far quicker, Milo: they won't just halve the population of the world, they will destroy it, globe and all. Meanwhile, one must do something to pass the time, so now to our muttons. My

* See *Blood of My Bone* by S. R. (Muller, 1989 or GraftonBooks)

information is that Carmilla and the rest of the Fatuous Four have gone to Narbonne, where they will follow up a heavy hint which they received at Montaillou the other day. So you will be pleased to hear, Milo, that you are now eating your last distressful dinner in Lourdes. Tomorrow we shall remove to an amusing hotel at Sète. It is right on the central canal and has an interior atrium with five circumjacent tiers of balconies leading to the bedrooms. A very handy place for suicide. An average of three fatalities, in the Icarus style, every month.'

'How very disagreeable. Shouldn't they arrange grilles or preventive netting?'

'Why? The French are much too sensible to deter anyone who wants to kill himself.'

'I meant, sir, disagreeable for the patrons of the hotel. One is sitting having a drink in this atrium, say, and some witless bankrupt or lover comes whizzing down SPLOSH at one's feet . . . or, worse still, on top of one's drink. But I suppose the place carries full insurance to replace it.'

'One can never tell with the French,' said Raisley Conyngham. 'In some matters they are unaccountably mean. I once left my shoes outside my door for cleaning – I was staying in a very civil hotel which offered that service – and they were ruined by some brute who filled them with piddle. The management refused to pay for them – they only took responsibility for property signed into the Hotel Safe, they said – as civil as ever. A pair handmade by Lobb, Milo. So perhaps we had better be careful, after arriving in Sète, where we sit in the hotel atrium. . . .'

'Dear Marius,' wrote Raisley Conyngham, who had discovered an entirely secure Writing Room (or *Chambre des Études*) just off the atrium in the *Auberge des Lan-goustes* at Sète:

Thank you for yrs. I'm indifferent about the death of that vulgar old woman, but very glad to *know* of it, as it raises one or two points which should be promptly made.

1) Mrs Malcolm's death should alter nothing in your relation to Teresa. On the one hand, she should still *not* be told that your father in wedlock was also hers from a chance bout with Maisie Malcolm; this disclosure could serve no sensible purpose and would almost certainly invalidate your option here, one that for a variety of good reasons should be allowed to remain open. On the other hand, although your option with Teresa should remain open, you are *not* to start dallying with her, if only because, as things are at present, this would annoy my Lady Canteloupe.

2) By extension, you are not to annoy anyone else either. You are to give no cause of complaint to anybody at all. You are to behave exactly as Henry VI commanded early pupils at his foundation of Eton College: '*Sitis boni pueri, mites et dociles, servientes Domino.*' You and I may have our own ideas as to which 'Dominus' you are in fact serving, but this must in no way be apparent to anyone else.

In brief, dear boy, mind your manners and mind your book . . . while I do battle (as I am now about to) with the busybodies and snoopers who would like to remove you from the range of my affection and influence.

Yours as ever,
Raisley Conyngham.

All of which is all very well, thought Marius Stern, when he read this letter at his school three days later, but I refuse to be taken for granted. I shall have to decide soon, decide for myself: Raisley Conyngham or Carmilla Salinger. It would go hard with me to separate myself from either, but harder, I think, to separate myself from Raisley . . . supposing, of course, that he would allow this, or could be compelled to withdraw. It is better to be owned by a man than by a woman: a man is generally civil enough not to insist orally on his right of ownership (even though he continues to exact it); a woman becomes shrill and nagging the moment one so much as forgets her birthday. But then again . . . perhaps Carmilla has more to offer than Raisley. Raisley purports to offer the world; Carmilla, like the Sirens, offers wisdom and resignation to necessity. True, this Sirens' song entices one towards a peace that may become torpor and, in the end, death. But even Raisley does not offer immortality, and such a gift would in any case be accursed. Does Raisley offer crowded hours of glorious life? Power? Fame? No. And rightly not. To be handed Power or Fame on a salver would be merely boring. Raisley offers something far more alluring. He offers to instruct one in such a manner that one can achieve power or fame by one's own efforts and therefore take the credit for oneself. Raisley offers the ultimate temptation: pride in personal attainment.

Well, thought Marius: I have no need to decide either way just yet. So meanwhile I shall accept Raisley's advice (telling myself that it is indeed advice rather than commandment), sit demure and still, let life go on, and gather minor merit.

It will be interesting to hear, later on, what is the result of this struggle (whatever form it may take) between Raisley and Carmilla in the Languedoc . . . The Languedoc, thought Marius: Troubadour Country. Jeremy says his father once heard a tale of an Englishman who went to Troubadour Country, where he learned the manner of the thing. Back in England, while he rode unarmed to a tryst, singing and playing to please his page, he was cut down by six black knights in full armour in a flowery meadow by a river. Fielding Gray was there when Jeremy repeated this story of his father's, and said that he – Fielding – had seen the grave of the troubadour, who was called Lord Geoffery of Underavon, in a Wiltshire churchyard. If Raisley is the leader of the Black Knights and Carmilla the troubadour, will Raisley cut her down with sword or lance? Or will she (just as the troubadour charmed his page) charm Raisley with her lute? Is it better to be cut down while singing to one's page in a flowery meadow by a river and then to rest in a churchyard in Wiltshire? Or is it better to be a Black Knight and ride home to the feast and the leman in one's castle?

The same day that Marius received Raisley Conyngham's letter, Carmilla, Jeremy, Fielding and Piero went to see the curator of the Museum of Antique Sculpture in the Priory Church in Narbonne. They had hoped to see him earlier, but the museum was closed from Friday noon to Monday noon, and the curator, who was called Jacques-Emile Gagneac, refused to grant them special audience, in the Priory Church or elsewhere, out of official museum hours.

'Hubertus Nivalis,' said Carmilla when they were all four seated opposite Gagneac (who used a princely sarcophagus as a desk and a chantry off the west end of the north aisle as an office), 'or Hubert Nivale, once of this city but interred at Montaillou, where he died. We have been told that further information about this Hubert may be available in this museum.'

'Oh yes,' said Jacques-Emile Gagneac: 'we of the Museum of Antique Sculpture are very interested in Hubert Nivale. We have acquired the right to the sarcophagus (it has a fascinating frieze on one side of it) in which the remains of his coffin were placed. Unfortunately the cost of transporting the sarcophagus from Montaillou to Narbonne is almost as massive as the sarcophagus itself, and our museum is not well primed with funds.'

He addressed this last remark towards the ceiling, where it hung in the barrel of the vaulting.

'*Quid pro quo*,' said Jeremy crisply. 'I shall be at charges, M. Gagneac, to transport the sarcophagus from Montaillou to the museum here in Narbonne, and you will be at pains to tell us what you know of Hubertus Nivalis Narbonnensis.'

'How refreshing to find an Englishman with whom it is easy to do business,' said Monsieur Gagneac.

'An English gentleman,' said Piero.

'No doubt that explains it,' said M. Gagneac sourly. 'Kindly come this way.'

He led them up the nave of the church and into the southern arm of the transept. Half-way along this was a screen of ten-foot high crudely constructed of loose chunks of marble, in the centre of which a narrow opening was guarded by a grille. This M. Gagneac unlocked and pulled back on villainously squeaking hinges.

'Our library,' he explained when they had all followed him through.

The term at first seemed grandiose, as there were no more than five shelves, on the south wall to the left of the south portal, that held books. But the slender collection became imposing when it was seen that every single volume was chained, roughly in the manner employed in the more celebrated library in Hereford Cathedral.

'Hubertus Nivalis was a merchant,' said Gagneac, 'whose money excited the greed of the Church and whose religious beliefs excited the curiosity of the Inquisition. His name figures frequently and prominently in the annals of the Inquisitorial Court presided over, from 1339 to 1351, by the Dominican Prior of the Priory of which this church was the centre. Hence the claim of the museum to the manuscript of the records – a manuscript which is, rather oddly for a legal document, very beautifully and eerily illustrated.'

He eased a large, long, fat volume into position on the desk above the shelf and began to turn the vellum pages. One by one he called up Carmilla and her following and showed each of them a picture of a richly dressed burgher of the fourteenth century, the lower part of whose robe had been cut away to reveal skeletal legs of ghastly luminous white.

'Hubert of Narbonne was given the sobriquet of "nivalis" or "snowy",' said the curator, 'because he was a leper. Since the disease attacked only his lower limbs – hence this disagreeable portrait – he was able to conceal the infection for some years. Normally, as a leper, he would have been turned adrift with a bell; as it was he was able to go about his business and (with discretion) his pleasures like any other man for some years . . . until, when he was in his late thirties, the disease started to gain ground and began to show slightly on his hands. These, of course, he kept gloved; yet eventually a servant discovered his debility and began to spread word – not plainly, for it was ill luck to name horrors such as leprosy, but in an easily comprehensible code: his master, he said, was "nivale" – "snowy".

'At this stage Hubert did something he had long planned to do: under pretence of going on a pilgrimage to the shrine at Roncevaux, he in fact took refuge in a household or *ostal* near Montaillou, owned by a business correspondent from Pamiers with whom he had long dealt in luxury imports which came in by Agde, Sète and Bacarès and were much prized by the inland nobility. The *ostal* had several advantages for Hubert: it was remote; it was inhabited by people who, like himself, were Black Cathars; it was near the source of some waters supposed to be efficacious even in cases of leprosy (these waters are still to be had at Molitq-les-Bains); and it was also near the church of a priest called Bertrand Cludes (Claudius in the Latin of the Court records) who was known, by the Cathars, to be secretly of their number and rumoured to possess miraculous powers of healing. However, Cludes-Claudius was a White Cathar and a "*perfectus*", i.e. one who had renounced all the goods and pleasures of this world. He told Hubert that in his opinion his leprosy, having long been dormant, was now about to spread over his entire body, and that like all leprosy it was beyond cure and in a few weeks would be beyond concealment – at which time he would have to be cast out by his kind and make his way, announcing his passage with his bell, to the nearest leper colony, which was in a forest near Foix. But Claudius had one helpful suggestion to make.'

Again Gagneac called up his audience, one by one, to examine an illustration from the Prior's Indictment: this was of a wasted figure, clearly *in extremis*, laid along a couch over which a cowled head was leaning in exhortation.

'Claudius offered Hubert the "*consolamentum*",' said Gagneac: 'a formula of prayer whereby a Cathar, or any man for that matter, is totally and eternally dedicated, by a White Cathar "*parfait*" or "*perfectus*", to the Good God, to the Pure and Celestial Faith, and so to assured Salvation, on these conditions: first, of absolute penitence for sins committed; and secondly, of what is called "the *endura*", which means complete abstinence from food or drink from the moment the "*consolamentum*" is finished until that of the penitent's death . . . which might, after all, be delayed by several days and thus make the "*endura*" live very painfully up to its name.

'In the end,' Gagneac continued, 'Hubert accepted this offer; but something then went very badly wrong. Although Cludes-Claudius waited several weeks, he had still badly miscalculated the time it would take Hubert to perish. Leprosy, even when flaring up after a long period of dormancy, is leisurely in its manner of killing. Hubert, penitent, fully purified by the White Cathar rites, all ready to inherit Salvation, simply did not die. Since he was permitted, and was given, nothing to eat or drink, he was in agony. The solution was obvious to anyone of charitable disposition: put the poor fellow out of his pain. Such a course was forbidden to White Cathars, so could not be followed by Claudius, who, however, raised no objection when Hubert's Black Cathar friends stifled him with a pillow. And there the matter would have been concluded, had not an informer from among the servants –'

'*Another* servant?' said Fielding Gray.

'It was the constant tactic of the ecclesiastical authorities to tempt servants to betray their masters,' said Jacques-Emile Gagneac, 'and the fees offered were generous. Hardly had Hubert's coffin been buried in a few inches of sun-baked earth (how it came to be housed in a sarcophagus is another story) than the Agents of the Inquisition were knocking on the portal of the *domus* in which he had died. His friends were all arrested – except the priest Cludes-Claudius, who had an accurate nose for trouble and had smelled it on the way back from the funeral. As a man of some consideration, he was on horseback; and when the group that had managed the burial was a mile or so from the *domus*, he suddenly turned his animal off the road and down a rough track which led away through the mountains in the direction of Perpignan. For many months, he was neither seen nor heard of again.'

Curator Gagneac beckoned to them one by one to take yet another look at the manuscript of the annals. This time there was a picture, exquisite in detail, of ramparts with towers and turrets at frequent intervals and one particularly prominent and complicated tower in the fore-ground. Near this were moored two thirteenth-century galleons, on to one of which some dispirited men-at-arms were embarking along an insecure gangway from an arched opening half-way up the near wall of Constance, as the tower was labelled.

'Aigues-Mortes,' said Fielding.

'Aigues-Mortes as it was then,' said Gagneac, 'when the sea, or rather the marine lagoon, came right up to the walls. Even now the area between Aigues-Mortes and the sea is mostly marsh and salt flat: in those days the only land was to be found in a group of Islets called Les Oiseaux, only the largest of which, Palus Dei (The Marsh of God) was inhabited. On this, which was little more than a bank of dunes encircling a quagmire of sea-mud, was a crude hamlet, from which a tiny colony of fishermen laboured for their livelihood and which was dominated by a three-storey keep of stone, the residence of the Seigneurs des Oiseaux, and a chapel adjacent to it very much of the kind you saw at Montaillou. Cludes – or Claudius – was a younger son of the reigning Seigneur, and hither he made his way, ferried by loyal tenants of his father's with whom he made contact while they were selling their catch at St-Gilles.

'But meanwhile, of course, the Inquisitors were on his trail . . . as was a party of vengeful Black Cathars who had heard how he had deserted their brothers near Montaillou and left them to be captured and tortured.'

'Surely, there was nothing much he could have done to help the wretches,' said Jeremy.

'It is no good expecting logic from peasants,' said Piero. 'Besides, it might have been expected of Cludes that whether he could help his companions or not he should have "gone up into Jerusalem", so to speak, "and perished with them".'

'His pursuers,' continued Gagneac, 'knew well enough who Claudius was and where they could probably find him. The problem was to procure passage. The narrow channels and submerged sandbanks of the dead waters were fatal to uninstructed mariners, and the only Masters of vessels capable of sailing there were the vassals of the Seigneur, who would on no account ferry strangers to their island, or the captains of the Royal Fleet, who only understood the possible courses directly south from Aigues-Mortes to the Mediterranean proper, whereas Les Oiseaux lay a league west by south of their harbour.'

'So,' said Carmilla, 'Claudius was safe home and immediately began, one imagines, to die of boredom.'

'He was a man of hardihood,' said Gagneac, 'and resource. Being a "perfect" he could survive without difficulty on fish or even, if pressed, on seaweed; and being not only a "perfect" but one of vision, he set himself to the task of designing and constructing his own tomb.

'This, he determined, should be cut into the inner south wall of the chancel of the chapel, next to some sedilia on which the family of the Seigneur habitually sat when attending Mass. The conception was prodigious. Cludes-Claudius set himself the task of depicting on the outside of his tomb the pure and original Cathar Cosmology as conceived by a *"parfait"* of the White Cathars. The carving, variously in high and low relief, was to show the creation of the Archangel Lucifer by God, the fall of Lucifer and his transformation into Satan – who, in his character of Demiurge, created the material universe, its stars and planets, and, at its centre, the Earth, on which human beings could revel in the pleasures Satan had concocted for them. It would also show an Allegorical Figure of the True (Cathar) Faith, who rejected the world and the flesh, lived a life of total asceticism, and finally assisted the Good God in the destruction of Satan and his

Universe. Cludes was busily engaged on this latter portion of his work when he was at last run to ground by an avenging posse of Black Cathars, who became even more vengeful when they saw Cludes' carving of their own Satan-God in the moment of defeat and humiliation. They murdered and dismembered the sculptor, threw the hideous framents to the sea birds, and were then themselves overcome and killed by the fisher-folk of the island, led by the Seigneur. Their bodies, together with that of the traitor who had guided them thither (once more, a servant) were burnt on the sea-shore and the ashes collected and placed in the hollow space behind the carven wall which had been intended by Cludes-Claudius as his own resting place. It was felt by his father to be an appropriate act of retribution to place the ashes of his enemies – cremation, remember, was rejected with horror by all Christians of the period, even by fundamental heretics – as a kind of trophy in the tomb which he himself could never occupy.'

'I see,' said Carmilla, as she looked again at the illustration of the Tower of Constance. 'So what began as the story of Hubertus Nivalis Narbonnensis ends in the story of the petty nobleman, Cludes-Claudius, on the Isle of Palus Dei.'

'The story ends,' said Gagneac, 'not with Cludes-Claudius in the intestines of the sea birds but with the carvings he made on the exterior of what he intended as his sepulchre. The carvings are still there, you know . . . a little worn after more than six hundred years, but easily discernible.'

'Is the Island approachable?' asked Fielding Gray.

'Very easily, these days. It is now in the centre of a small lagoon, which one crosses on a causeway.'

'A tourist attraction, one supposes?' said Jeremy.

'No,' said Gagneac. 'The indigenous inhabitants of

Palus Dei, who still make a livelihood, a very wretched one, from fishing, are as hostile to strangers now as they were six hundred years ago. Now as then they still profess the faith of White Cathars (several of them being "perfects"). Since the population is by now the result of incestuous unions, there is a high level of insanity, which reveals itself in a fanatical adherence to their faith, the centre of which is Cludes-Claudius's monument to its Cosmology. The tomb is so zealously guarded that even if a stranger made his way safely over the causeway he would be expelled – or worse – long before he came within sight of the chapel. You should understand,' said Gagneac, 'that the Island is totally beyond the administration and without the law. The bureaucracy and the police have simply agreed to leave it alone, to thrive or perish as it will. Since it is extremely remote – the causeway which leads to it begins in the middle of a wilderness of giant reeds and sea-grasses, which in turn can only be approached through a marsh by a secret track two miles long – it is not likely to be discovered.'

'How do they live, these islanders?' enquired Piero.

'By the fish which they catch. They ceased to sell any of it "on the mainland" a good hundred and fifty years ago, when the Gendarmerie first began to show an interest (since abandoned, as I say) in Palus Dei. Their diet of fish is supplemented by various roots and flora found in the mire at the centre of the Island. For the rest, well, they have few needs, and these are catered for by the household articles pillaged from the Donjon when the Seigneurial family died out in the nineteenth century.'

'When one considers the condition and situation of Palus Dei,' said Carmilla, 'one is surprised that you appear to know so much about it.'

'There is an English student of these affairs,' said Jacques-Emile-Gagneac, 'a scholar called Conyngham.

His main interest is in scattered examples of the survival of Black Cathars, but he is also interested in the White, who are far rarer. He has access to Palus Dei because he has shown, to the satisfaction of the fishermen, that his ancestors were related to the Seigneurs of Les Oiseaux. Since the islanders are loyal to their former lords, they are disposed, besides making use of their furniture and other effects which they left, to be civil to their kin. M. Conyngham, with whom I have the honour to be slightly acquainted, visits Palus Dei from time to time and engages in a close study of the Cludes-Claudius monument.'

'Surely,' said Jeremy, 'there is a limit to the amount of "study" which these carvings will justify?'

'There is a mystery,' said Gagneac, 'which has never been solved. Next to the carvings, at the far end of them, which illustrated the defeat of the Devil, is a panel which guards the entrance to the hollow interior, which was originally intended for the dead body of Cludes-Claudius.'

'And now contains what is left, if anything, of the ashes of his murderers?'

'Correct,' said the curator. 'On this panel is engraved a small Maltese Cross. At first M. Conyngham thought that this had been carved by Cludes-Claudius to signify the descent of the Seigneurs, and so of himself, from noblemen of Malta. Then he realized that any such reference would have been made by a representation of quarterings or some other heraldic insignia, such as a crest. And then he also realized, on close examination, that the Cross was of a far later period than the carvings made by Cludes-Claudius.'

'Perhaps the carving of the Cross was made by another member of the family?' suggested Fielding Gray.

'No. Close inspection shows that this carving, though contrived to look ancient, was in fact made after, long after, the demise of the last Seigneur and the cessation of the family.'

'Exactly when?' said Carmilla.

'That is what M. Conyngham is trying to determine. Unfortunately he is not expert in matters of sculpture.'

'But you yourself?' said Jeremy, gesturing beyond the screen to indicate the museum at large, full of carven and engraved stone. 'You yourself would surely be able to date such work?'

'I am an expert in *ancient* sculpture. This Maltese Cross would appear to be modern. But I might be of help, if I could see the work and examine it. And at last, M. Conyngham writes from England, he has thought of a way for me . . . and others . . . to gain access to the Island. You have seen the little tablet in the Sarcophagus of Hubert Nivale?'

'Yes.'

'We do not know when his coffin was put into the sarcophagus, but we may assume that the tablet was put there at the same time. Whoever placed the coffin there must have done so because it was in bad repair, and he would therefore have been able to notice that there was no little black figure at the inside head of it – an omission almost certainly insisted on by the White Cathar, Cludes-Claudius, who had administered the "*consolamentum*" to Hubert. Besides, records kept by the Black Cathars probably helped Hubert's benefactor to realize what was to be expected of Hubert's coffin. And so, knowing that Hubert was in fact a Black Cathar but had been nagged into accepting the rites of the White, our man doubtless caused a tablet to be carved with Hubert's name, a suitable inscription and the little black figure, and placed it in the sarcophagus with the coffin.'

'Possibly,' said Carmilla. 'What has this to do with gaining safe access to Palus Dei?'

'First of all,' said Gagneac, 'one must know the route. Of this I have a map made by M. Conyngham.'

'And what of your reception when you arrived?'

'If one took with one a similar tablet to that which commemorates Hubert, and on it one had carved the name of one of the very early Seigneurs of Les Oiseaux, who in fact died away from the islands, in St-Gilles, say, on one of the commercial expeditions there, and if one also carved on it an inscription *and*, in this case, a tiny upright figure, inlaid in white, of a White Cathar at prayer, then it is at least possible that those who came bearing such a memorial and a plausible tale to explain it might be admitted on to the Island. The islanders are very proud of being White Cathars and of having a line of rulers (albeit now defunct) who had been Cathars from the time of the origin of the heresy – to them, of course, the true faith. Such a gift would call for a reward, and if the reward one asked was to be allowed to visit the great Tomb carved by Cludes-Claudius, it could hardly be refused.'

'And then,' said Carmilla, 'one could examine this mysterious and apparently modern Maltese Cross and perhaps deduce its provenance?'

'Precisely,' said Jacques-Emile Gagneac.

'The trouble is,' said Carmilla, 'that one is not knowledgeable in this field. You are not, as you admit; and I am not; and these gentlemen are not.'

'Five pairs of eyes, looking with a fresh gaze, might perceive something,' said Gagneac.

'The faked tablet of which you speak – '

' – I have one in my office – '

' – would be an adequate *laissez-passer* for all five of us?'

'I am prepared to chance it if you are. To look at this remarkable Tomb – that would be a privilege,' said

173

Gagneac. 'And to deduce something about this mysterious modern Cross would be a minor triumph of scholarship. I think all of us here have the spirit of scholars. I think so simply because we *are* here.'

'I should certainly like to see that sepulchre,' said Piero Caspar.

'I should certainly like to get to that Island,' said Fielding Gray.

'A new and unknown world,' said Jeremy Morrison.

'An old and unknown world,' corrected Carmilla Salinger.

Raisley Conyngham and Milo Hedley sat in Le Jardin de la Fountain at Nîmes. Pines and cedars gave them shade and shelter (both most grateful, for it was one of the occasional hot and windy winter days in the city), lawns and terraces and balustrades gave them repose and delight of the spirit, and a noble swan, whose constant efforts to take off into the air from a pond below a cascade were constantly frustrated by the cruel debility of his clipped wings, provided Raisley with matter for moralizing.

'That poor bird,' he said, 'does not understand what has been done to it nor that it can never fly again. So it will keep trying, quite in vain, for the rest of its life. Similarly, Carmilla and her cronies do not understand the limitations imposed by a rational education upon their mind and mood of thought. They will never be able to conceive of a world that is not governed by Newtonian notions of cause and effect. They do not belong to the age of Relativity and the Quantum Theory. They know about them of course, but they conceive of them only in three-dimensional and mechanical terms. The metaphysical and supernatural implications are beyond them.'

'Piero Caspar,' said Milo, 'has not been maimed and limited by a rational education. His childhood in Sicily taught him all about the supernatural, or so Provost Llewyllyn told me when I stayed with him last summer.'

'Piero has had his share of rational education since he commenced as an undergraduate at Lancaster. During all that time his old instinctive knowledge of the pagan gods, whether oppidan or silvan, has been eroded. Like Carmilla, Major Gray and your erstwhile catamite, Jeremy Morrison, Piero Caspar (not for nothing promoted Fellow of his college) expects everything to be explicable in the terms of classical statics and dynamics . . . though of course he may retain some residual tags of his old knowledge. But like the rest of them, Piero is now propelled by two motives: first by curiosity, *not* so much to discover a solution to a problem or a mystery, but to see in what manner that solution ultimately fits in, however eerie or non-worldly the circumstances, with his strictly rational preconceptions; and second by vanity, the self-satisfaction derived from being clever enough to solve a mystery and from finding that the answer, as he has always maintained it would be, is rendered in a logical and natural frame. You see, Milo, whatever the true answer is, such people will always re-model it till it appears to accord with such a frame.'

'So to curiosity and vanity we add intellectual dishonesty?'

'We can do so if we wish. But curiosity and vanity, Milo, will be quite enough to serve our turn. Now then. Carmilla & Co. have been invited to accompany an old ally of mine on a visit to an obscure island in the Camargue on which is situated rather a remarkable tomb. They have been told there is a mystery about the tomb – a mystery that can be cleared up by the application of their knowledge, culture and intelligence. Inevitably, the appeal to curiosity and vanity has led them to accept the invitation. But suppose, Milo, just suppose, that the mystery turns out, after all, to have a supernatural or larval solution? Or at any rate to appear, beyond confutation, to have one?'

'If they are convinced, they will be very put out.'

'Precisely. So put out, that from now on they may make themselves scarce and mind their own business, in this and indeed in all other matters.'

'It will certainly throw them off their stroke, sir,' Milo said.

'I hope so. I am getting very bored with their interference. You will accompany me to see what happens when they are confronted by . . . by whatever will confront them?'

'I wouldn't want to miss it, sir.'

'Good. Now we shall return to Sète to rest before this adventure. You have brought some really warm clothes with you?'

'Warmish. Nothing for the Arctic.'

'The damp cold of the marshes is more treacherous if not so savage as that of the Arctic. We shall buy you something appropriate before we leave Nîmes.'

'Something in fur, sir?'

'Something drab but effective from French Army surplus, if we can find the right shop.' Raisley rose. 'The military do things very well, Milo, when they turn their minds to them. Almost anything. For example, these beautiful gardens. Few people realize that they were the creation of an eighteenth-century Army engineer.'

'It does say so, sir, here in the Green Michelin.'

'Yes. But the artist gets a brief phrase, where Capability Brown would get a paragraph, and he is not named. That is because the kind of people who write guide books, Milo, hate the military and virulently grudge them credit. They do not willingly acknowledge even that soldiers fight on their behalf during wars. Still less do they give proper

176

praise to a soldier for an endeavour – look around you, Milo – that belongs (they think) only to their own kind. When confronted with such a phenomenon, they become truculent and evasive. In rather the same way, Carmilla and her chums will become truculent and evasive when confronted with an instance of the supernatural. They will be *shamed* into silence.'

'I don't think that any of them,' said Milo, 'was ever shamed into anything.'

'They will be frightened into silence.'

'That lot don't scare easily.'

'Then they will be,' said Raisley Conyngham, '*compelled* into silence.'

'Ah,' said Milo: 'there, sir, speaks my Master.'

'Since we are complete strangers to the islanders,' Carmilla Salinger said to Jacques-Emile Gagneac, 'is it altogether sensible to arrive after dusk?'

'The men are out all day fishing,' said Gagneac: 'the women are even more ferocious and even less literate than the males. A stranger's best chance of being properly understood lies in his presenting himself to the Head Man of the hamlet. Or so I am instructed by M. Conyngham from England.'

'With this tablet,' said Carmilla, examining it. 'I see you have made a very distinctive job of the praying white figure; and I also see you have chosen a very apposite epitaph for the Seigneur: "*Animae Sanctorum sunt in manu Dei.*" "The souls of the righteous are in the hand of God." Let us hope the Head Man speaks Latin.'

'Heretics, like true Catholics, used to pray in Dog Latin,' said Jacques-Emile; 'the modern mode of using the vernacular will not yet have disturbed Palus Dei.'

* * *

'Here are the sedilia,' said Raisley Conyngham to Milo Hedley; 'and this is the tomb which was carved for himself by the priest and White Cathar, Cludes-Claudius – the tomb which, as I explained to you on the way here, is in fact occupied by the ashes of his murderers, the body of Cludes himself having been thrown piecemeal to *les oiseaux* of Les Oiseaux. There is the panel that conceals the hollow space within, intended to contain a cadaver; and there' – he carried his torch closer to the panel – 'is the Maltese Cross, which Carmilla and her group are coming to investigate.'

'The Cross which looks old?'

'As you can see,' said Raisley.

'But was in fact carved pretty recently.'

'Correct.'

'What do we do now, sir?'

'Sedilia, as even a Trinity man knows, are for sitting on. So we shall sit on them and wait. We are here, by design, a good hour before Gagneac will arrive with our opponents. I shall switch off the torch to save the battery. You do not mind waiting in the dark?'

'Not with you, sir, for you are a Lord of it.'

'Do I detect a hint of irony, Milo? Have a care, boy, have a care. So. Here we are, comfortably settled on the sedilia. I extinguish the torch – thus – and now I shall a tale unfold to beguile you while we wait.'

'Another tale, sir?'

'Yes, Milo. Another. I trust you will not find it tedious. I have told you how the priest/Cathar Cludes-Claudius administered the "*consolamentum*" to Hubert Nivale, how Hubert, taking too long to die his agonizing death, was suffocated by his friends, how these friends were arrested on their return from Hubert's funeral, and how Cludes-Claudius, scenting trouble, deserted them on their way back to the *ostal*, and escaped to this Island. All this, of course, has also been told to Carmilla and her boys by Gagneac . . . who is bringing them here, pretending they need a false token to satisfy the islanders (to make the matter more circumstantially complicated and thus more convincing to the rational mind), not having told them that all the islanders have long since died or departed, and that the place is deserted. Now, what Gagneac has not told the gang of four, and what I have not yet told you, is what happened to the corporal remains of Hubert Nivale. They know and you know that his coffin was hurriedly buried. They know and you know that at some stage a well-wisher placed the rotting coffin inside a magnificent pagan sarcophagus, together with a tablet to identify the coffin's occupant. But what neither they know or you know is what has become of that occupant.'

'In six hundred years, sir? Dust to dust.'

'No, no, Milo. How worthless the education they purvey at Trinity these days. Or is it just you who is unworthy? Either way, Milo, pray attend to this: the skeleton, the "steadfast and enduring bone" (as Housman has it), can go on for millennia. Have they not taught you that in the Schools?'

'The matter hardly comes within my curriculum.'

'It used to come within Dean ffoliott-Hume's curriculum. It was one of his hobbies.'

'I do not attend tutorials, sir, with Dean ffoliott-Hume.'

'No more you do. How silly of me to assume, simply because the good Dean is among my acquaintance, that you would be up to him for your studies. Never mind. You will doubtless accept my assurance (and Housman's) that bones do indeed endure; and you will doubtless be inquisitive to know what became of those of Hubert Nivalis Narbonnensis.'

'Anything you say, sir.'

'A little more enthusiasm, Milo, please. We have

179

walked a long way, I know, through marsh and wilderness and along a crumbling causeway to get here; but do not let fatigue dull your attention when our affair is approaching its climax.'

'Sorry, sir. Of course I am burning to know what happened to the skeletal remains of Hubertus.'

'Let us not have any false zeal either,' said Raisley Conyngham: 'just intelligent interest.'

'Sir.'

'Well then. Hubert's skeleton was purloined, we shall never know by whom, in order to serve as a fetish or auspicious relic for the community of Black Cathars (few in number yet finite) that still survive in the area of Montaillou and Molitq-les-Bains. Gagneac has seen it and so have I. In fact it was our suggestion that so precious an object of reverence should be concealed somewhere really remote and obscure (instead of the chest it occupied in a farmhouse near Prades) – should indeed be moved to this Island of Palus Dei.'

'Not very fitting, sir, if I may say so. The islanders were White Cathars; Hubert was Black.'

'Oh yes, indeed. Hubert, one might say, was the Red Gold from a Black Tomb. And now, so near him, the Seigneurs of Les Oiseaux and their fisher-folk vassals rest in the white graves we passed on the way to this chapel. Nevertheless, you will agree that this place, of any in France, is secure. No busybody – no historian nor archaeologist nor archivist nor bureaucrat nor health inspector – will come on Hubert Nivale's skeleton here in the Marsh of God.'

'Exactly *where*, sir, in the Marsh of God? Here in the Tomb which Claudius carved?'

'Precisely: this Tomb, constructed indeed by a White Cathar but occupied by the ashes of Black ones, the friends of Hubert's friends who buried him, the men that

180

had murdered Cludes for his cowardly desertion of the burial party.'

'And the Maltese Cross . . . behind which Hubert lies?'

'A typical Maltese Cross, Milo . . . a symbol often regarded as an evil omen, as a warning which says, "Keep out, do not pry", or, in this case, "Accursed be he that violates this panel".'

'You and Gagneac violated it to place Hubert inside the Tomb.'

'No, Milo. We found the Cross among bric-a-brac in Gagneac's museum. We battered it about and affixed it to the panel – with the assistance of a powerful industrial glue – *after* we had deposited Hubert inside.'

'To warn off . . . whom, sir?' Milo said. 'You yourself told me that nobody will come here meaning harm to Hubert's skeleton.'

'To warn off ghosts of the islanders. They placed the ashes of Cludes's murderers inside as a kind of trophy; but that is not to say that they would tolerate, in this Chapel, the entire skeleton of a Black Cathar (even of one who had received the "*consolamentum*") that had been wished on them by other Black Cathars. And indeed it is this insult to the dead islanders that will make for the scene of the supernatural that will so dismay Carmilla and company. They will see the ghosts of the fishermen of Palus Dei hovering around this panel, meaning hatred and harm to Hubert within it, but frustrated and barred from entry by the emblem of the Maltese Cross, and at last withdrawing in misery and rage. They come every night, these ghosts, Milo – or that is what Gagneac will tell Carmilla and her band of brothers.'

'A chilling tale,' said Milo, unchilled.

'You know it. They do not. They think they are coming here to carry out an archaeological investigation. Only when they are here will Gagneac tell them the true

181

significance of the Maltese Cross and what they will shortly witness.'

'And where shall we be, sir?'

'By the altar, listening. Unseen, watching and listening.'

Jeremy, thought Milo. My catamite, my darling, one to whom I must make love no more, Raisley says, in case of this new American and African disease. Nevertheless, one can love one's darling without making love. I love you, Jeremy, my creature, my bugger-boy, my own sweet sweeting. You and your lovely round buttocks and your lovely round face. Your low and soothing voice. Your presence, the soft sweet touch of your hand, your words of lust, your words of grace. And now I am to see you made a fool of by Conyngham and his ghosts. Raisley, my Master: Jeremy, my pathic darling, heart of the heart of my heart.

'The Demiurge,' said Jacques-Emile Gagneac, flashing his torch on to a carved figure, naked, sinuous, and negroid in feature, that was emitting galaxies in streams from the tips of all eight fingers. 'The Earth,' said Gagneac, plying his torch; 'the Pleasures of the Flesh' – these apparently being a girdle round the Earth of infants in suggestive conjunction.

'It reminds me of Huxley's *Brave New World*,' said Fielding Gray. 'Children engaged in erotic play.'

'You see,' whispered Raisley to Milo, as they crouched beside the altar: 'Vanity – the desire to demonstrate knowledge and wide reading.'

'It will be interesting,' Milo replied, 'to see how they demonstrate their knowledge when Gagneac comes on to the Maltese Cross.'

'As a matter of fact,' Raisley muttered back, 'they won't get a chance. Remember: the invitation to play the expert is a mere ruse to get them here; their attention will be fully occupied by something quite different.'

'Oh yes,' said Milo: 'the rancorous ghosts of the dead fishermen, vainly seeking entry to the interior of the Tomb.'

'They may, of course, fail to show up,' said Raisley; 'ghosts, you know, are not absolutely dependable.'

'Then Carmilla and her lads will have had a long walk for nothing.'

'Yes,' said Raisley: 'a long walk ending in nothing. Quiet now: let us listen to what they are learning from Gagneac.'

'The Day of Doom for Satan the Demiurge,' said Gagneac, playing his torch on the rippling body of the Creator, which was being stretched on a rack by Harpies and Sirens as it gradually floated down to where more Harpies were raising their claws to receive it.

'A Nest of Harpies in Hell,' said Gagneac. 'And now the Maltese Cross which you have come to examine. With an addition hitherto unadvertised: watch for the spirits of the dead . . . with which you will soon be confronted.'

For about two seconds the beam of the torch lit a black cross which resembled a miniature four-pronged airscrew, with blades about nine inches long and amputated where they began to narrow to the tip.

Just like the Other Ranks' cap-badge of the 60th Rifles, thought Fielding, probably snatched from a Memorial to the Green Jackets in a War Cemetery in Italy or the north of France, and then hacked about a bit.

Before he could communicate this opinion or confirm it by further inspection, the torch went out.

'What's the trouble, M. Gagneac?' said Carmilla.

There was no answer.

'Come,' whispered Raisley to Milo, and guided him through a gap in the apsidal wall at the rear of the Chapel.

'What's going on?' Milo heard Jeremy call plaintively.

Other expostulations from Carmilla and her group grew fainter as Raisley and Milo moved swiftly along the dunes, the lagoon being on their right and the quagmire on their left, towards the old harbour of Palus Dei, from which the causeway now ran across the lagoon towards the distant wilderness of sea-grass.

'You see?' said Raisley. 'Even if a man kept by the sea and avoided the morass; even if he negotiated, in the pitch dark, the crumbling causeway; even if he found, at the heart of the wilderness of sea-grasses, the beginning of the path which leads away through the marsh to the distant road, he would still have to find his way along that path. It is designed, at every turning, to pitch any way-farer strange to it into the quicksands. They will indeed be confronted by the spirits of the dead – if any such there be – before the night is out.'

'They will pass a very cold and uncomfortable night, Raisley,' said Milo, 'and come out by daylight.'

'If they stay there all night they may die of exposure.'

'They are young, Raisley, and they have each other to embrace for warmth.'

'Even if they wait for day and are still alive when it dawns, they will never find the path from the wilderness, and even if they find it they will never reach the end of it. It was still light when you and I came along that path to get here. Did you notice how often I had to pause, how often even I was nearly thrown into the black bog? So when and if they leave this island, Milo, they will very soon begin, as I told you, to mind their own business and cease interfering with my plans for Marius. Can you see the headlines? "Tragic disappearance of English explorers amid uncharted waters".'

'There will not only be headlines, Raisley,' said Milo as

Raisley led him along the treacherous causeway: 'there will be enquiries.'

'Yes. Weeks or months later. After they find – if indeed they ever do – what is left of Carmilla and her trusting wolf cubs. No one will have known they were coming here, Milo: Gagneac impressed on them the need for secrecy, lest there were to be official prohibition. No one will have seen them set out in the dark with Gagneac. No one will know or care where you and I were going when we left the hotel at Sète or where we have been when we return to it.'

'Marius will smell something amiss when he hears that they have disappeared.'

'Marius is sworn to obey me, Milo. So are you.'

'Yes. Yes indeed, sir. The sooner we get back to Sète and some supper, the happier I shall be in my obedience.'

'There spake my loyal Apprentice.'

'There spake my Worshipful Master.'

'If we keep our heads,' said Carmilla, 'which, I may say, we have not done hitherto, we shall come out of this without trouble.'

No one liked to mention that that might not be too easy in view of the perilous and little-known route which they would have to follow. Piero, however, felt it worth remarking that they had a very cold, damp night in front of them, whatever else.

'Movement is the thing to keep one warm,' Jeremy said.

'No one is to move anywhere until we have light to move by,' said Carmilla, in an officer voice.

Jeremy was about to remark that the movements he had in mind were perfectly compatible with safely remaining exactly where they were, but decided, on second thoughts, that he would only be most roundly snubbed by

Carmilla, in her present mood, presumably on the ground that energy must not be frivolously expended.

'In the Army,' said Fielding Gray, 'we used to sing to keep warm at night. Hymns, bawdry, anything that came to mind.'

'Making things dead easy for the enemy,' said Jeremy: 'I always thought that regiment of yours was a pretty amateur affair.'

'When there was an enemy to be avoided,' said Fielding, 'we did silent exercises.' Now you're talking, thought Jeremy. 'Like curling and uncurling the fingers, very slowly,' Fielding went on. 'You'd be surprised how effective it is.'

'For the fingers, no doubt,' said Jeremy. 'What about the rest of one?'

'Proceed on the same principle, *mutatis mutandis*. Knees bend, press-ups, flexing of the stomach.'

'Now that sounds promising,' said Jeremy in an arch voice.

'I want no lubricious insinuations out of you, Jeremy Morrison,' said Carmilla like a female Savonarola faced with Botticelli's Venus. 'There is a time and a place for everything, and this shrine, albeit at present invisible, is no place for that sort of sacrilege.'

'You never objected to that sort of sacrilege in Ely Cathedral,' Jeremy said, 'in Bishop Alcock's Chantry. You squealed fit to raise him from the dead.'*

'You unspeakable cad,' snorted Carmilla.

'At least,' said Piero, in order to change the topic, 'we now know that we did right to come here to the Languedoc. We must have been very close to Conyngham's secrets for him to arrange our demise.'

'We are not interested,' said Carmilla rather grandly,

* See *Morning Star* by S. R. (Muller, Blond & White, 1984 or GraftonBooks)

'in the possibility of demise. First things first. Getting through the night. Singing, as Fielding suggests. I'll begin:

' "Who would true valour see," ' she chanted throatily.

' "Let him come hither . . ." '

The men lifted up their voices and followed her in the old song:

' "One here will constant be,
Come wind, come weather . . ." '

About a furlong from a minor but tolerable road the path across the marshes mounted on to solid ground and became an easy and ordinary track.

'I'm quite glad that's over,' Raisley Conyngham said, switching off his torch as they climbed into his car. 'Incidentally, I noticed that you called me "Raisley" instead of "sir" once or twice back on the Island. I thought we agreed that this was not to happen until you emerged from your apprenticeship.'

'For a moment or two, sir, I thought that I had emerged. But then common sense asserted itself.'

'And what made you think,' said Raisley, turning the car right on to the main road for Sète via Montpelier, 'what made you think, Milo, even for a moment or two, that you had emerged from your apprenticeship?'

'If one has been made privy to a conspiracy to murder four people, one could be said – one just could be said – to have grown out of the status of mere apprentice.'

'Not unless one has actually seen at least one of them die.'

'That is what occurred to me, sir; so I resumed the condition of apprentice and renewed calling you "sir".'

'Your education has a long way to go yet, Milo. Not only, as I have just observed, have you never witnessed actual death by murder, but you are entirely ignorant of death by Anathema.'

'Anathema, sir?'

'The Curse of God, or (to loyal Black Cathars) the Curse of Satan, who is also God.'

'Are you a Black Cathar, sir? You know some of them, that is evident, and you are interested in their doctrine, but are you actually one of them?'

'I am eclectic, Milo,' Raisley Conyngham said: 'I make use of whatever faith, philosophy or formula I fancy at the time. I have recently chosen to place the Anathema of Satan on my house and estate at Ullacote. You know why?'

'No, sir. It seems rather an unreasonable proceeding.'

'There speaks the apprentice, you see. Understand, Milo: this Curse will affect anyone who has ever stayed at Ullacote – anyone, that is, of my selection. You and Marius have stayed there; you are both, of course, exempt from the Curse.'

'And Teresa Malcolm, sir?'

'Also exempt. So long as Teresa is close to Theodosia Canteloupe, we may well need her. We no longer need Captain Jack Lamprey and we no longer need Gat-Toothed Jenny, the stable lass. Both, as you know, are dead.'

'Simply because you no longer need them, sir?' Milo enquired demurely.

'No. Because I was sorry for them. I exercise more human pity than you might think. Lamprey had before him only drunken stupors and a steady decline in his skill with horses, the one thing that made life worthwhile for him. Jenny was possessed of a yearning for Marius, which would have been answered only with his total neglect when absent and his blistering scorn when present.'

'And yet he loved her once.'

'Briefly. With my consent . . . which was withdrawn as soon as Jenny had served her turn.'

'And you claim to exercise human pity?'

'Jenny had an hour or two of ecstatic happiness. This is more than falls to the lot of most of us. The price – early death – is trivial. Any wise person would in any case prefer an early death, when he or she considers the horrors that life probably has in store.'

'Still . . . he or she might wish, sir, to make the choice for him- or herself.'

'That is mere self-regarding folly, and need not even be reckoned.'

'So who else that has been at Ullacote will be victim of your Curse?'

'The horse, Lover Pie. He holds attractive memories for Marius of his childhood innocence. These memories I wished to exploit when I made Marius his stable lad at Ullacote last April.* Now I wish to blot them out.'

'Why?' asked Milo.

The car, which had been skirting Montpelier, veered left at a sign marked

FRONTIGNAC
SÈTE

'They are memories, not only of the horse, but of Jeremy Morrison; memories of a soft spring day some three or four years ago† when they went to Newmarket together and backed Lover Pie, who won his race at thirty-three to one. At that time he belonged to someone other than myself.'

'So you are jealous that Marius backed Lover Pie and won money on him before the horse belonged to you?'

'No, Milo. I am jealous of Marius' memories of that

---

* See *Before the Cock Crow* by S. R. (Muller, Blond & White, 1986 or GraftonBooks)
† See *Morning Star* by S. R. (Muller, Blond & White, 1984 or GraftonBooks)

day and other days with Jeremy Morrison . . . because they are memories of happiness and, as I say, of innocence.'

'Say also of "love", sir. Jeremy inspires a lot of love.'

'Most of all I am jealous of that love,' Raisley Conyngham said.

'I understand, sir. I hope the head waiter has paid proper attention to our supper. Walking across that marsh is hungry work.'

'"But there's another country,"' sang Carmilla and her band, '"Which I heard of long ago – "'

The wind, shrill-chill, blew along the chapel, drowning the next few lines –

'"Oh, you may not count her armies,"' they sang as the wind faltered,

> And you may not see her king,
> For her fortress is a faithful heart
> And her pride is suffering;
> But hour by hour and silently
> Her shining bounds increase,
> And her ways are ways of pleasantness
> And all her paths are peace.

'Those last lines again,' called Piero.

'I am sorry to interrupt,' said Milo Hedley, his torchlit face suddenly appearing bodiless before them, 'but the sooner we leave this the better.'

'Milo,' said Jeremy.

'Jeremy,' said Milo.

'Surely it is better to wait for the light,' said Carmilla.

'No. I have walked the path between the wilderness and the road both in light and darkness. It is easier, provided one has a torch, at night. Easier and less frightening; for you do not see what is around you and you can concentrate harder on what is at your feet. Besides, I must get back before Raisley wakes. I came as soon as he had finished supper and gone to bed. When he wakes – which will be early – he will come to my room to look for me. He is a lonely man, you see.'

'He will guess that you came for us when he hears we are safe,' said Fielding.

'You are not safe yet,' Milo said.

'He will have no proof that it was Milo who saved us,' said Jeremy.

'If he does save us,' Piero said. 'Given that, Mr Conyngham, as Major Gray says, will guess.'

'Follow the torch carefully,' said Milo, as he led the way from the chapel to the dunes.

While they filed along the dunes, Milo continued to speak. As he spoke, Fielding remembered the old film *Ivanhoe* and how the Templar Knight (George Sanders) said that to betray his master in the combat that was to come would cost him his knighthood and probably his life, in any case his spurs and his honour, but all this he would gladly abandon for the love of Rebecca. It seemed to Fielding that Milo was saying somewhat of this kind, save that it was not knighthood and honour that he imperilled but the grace and favour of Raisley Conyngham (which to Milo was all his honour), and that it was not for love of Rebecca the Jewess that he would be content to forfeit these things but for love of Jeremy Morrison. This is what, as it seemed to Fielding, Milo Hedley was saying in the sand dunes.

While they walked along the causeway Milo was silent, using his torch carefully to help each one of them, but when they came to the wilderness of sea-grasses, he spoke again:

'In any case,' he said, 'Raisley Conyngham would eventually cast me off, as he does everybody in the end.

Poor old ffoliott-Hume of Trinity, and sozzler Jack Lamprey, and steadfast Jenny, and the brave stallion, Lover Pie. He will even cast off Marius, at the last, curse him and cast him off, when he has tired of him or Marius has displeased him. He has a belief, has Raisley, in the power of his curses. Never mind whether this belief is justified or not, what he wishes has a way of coming to pass.'

'Not tonight,' Piero said.

'He has been thwarted tonight,' said Milo, 'because his apprentice has been false to him. He will know this, as Major Gray says. Even if he does not destroy me, he will disown me. I shall no longer be his apprentice, so I shall no longer be able, since I shall no longer have privileged knowledge of his plans, to defy him. I cannot help you save Marius. I do not care for Marius as I care for Jeremy, but nevertheless I wish him to be saved. Here is the beginning of the path: watch the torch closely. If we come safely through the marsh, return at once to England and preserve Marius Stern from Raisley Conyngham.'

'How shall we do that?' said Carmilla Salinger.

'In the same way as I am rescuing Jeremy. It may be that to save Marius you will have to lose or forfeit or abandon – or even betray – something or somebody else that is very dear to you. I wonder which, if any, of you is ready to do that?'